QUEEN
OF THE
NIGHT

N.OWENS

DEDICATION

THIS ONE IS FOR THE ONES WHO
DON'T THINK THEY CAN FIND
THEIR ONE (OR ONE'S) JUST WAIT
BABE. SOMEONE WILL LOVE YOUR
CRAZY ASS FOR WHO YOU ARE.

ALSO HUGE SHOUT OUT TO MY
CRAZY RED HEAD BESTIE. GIRL,
THIS BOOK WASN'T GONNA GET
DONE IF NOT FOR YOU.
THANK YOU!

TABLE OF CONTENTS

TABLE OF CONTENTS

TRIGGER WARNING

PLEASE READ POSSIBLE TRIGGERS
BEFORE CONTINUING. YOUR MENTAL
HEALTH IS IMPORTANT TO ME.

THIS IS A DARK ROMANCE BOOK
CONTAINING SOME DARK THEMES.

SEXUAL INTERACTIONS
POSSESSIVE MMC
IMPLIED SA
PRAISE KINK
VIOLENCE
KIDNAPPING

IF THIS IS YOUR THING.
PLEASE CONTINUE ON...

CHAPTER ONE

TRINITY

"Dad! Stop! You're hurting her. Please stop!" My dad shakes my mom aggressively, as if she were a rag doll, as I stand there in horror, pleading for him to stop. I had just gotten home from taking a walk in the woods behind our run-down house. I was taking pictures for my portfolio and thought a nature section would look cool. Dad was still at work when I left, and Mom was once again zoned out on the couch, staring at the television. I think she took pills again, but it doesn't matter. I just need to survive this place for three more years, and then I'm gone. Anywhere but this hellhole will work.

"You stupid bitch. You fucked him for drugs again, didn't you? You're a fucking whore." Slap. I wince at the sound of my dad's palm landing across my mother's cheek. This is a regular occurrence under this roof, but Dad seems more unhinged than usual tonight. I can smell the booze coming off him in waves and know that tonight is going to end in a beating for me as well. He needs power over everyone. Even if I kept my mouth shut and hid in my room, he would find a way to punish me for something.

My bedroom light is on. I'm wasting power. A dish in the sink. I'm a freeloader and need to learn my place. Heaven forbid I stick up for my junkie mother. I'm a whore just like her, spreading my legs for every man in this godforsaken town just to embarrass him. Doesn't matter that I'm still a virgin and never even thought a boy in this town was worth my time.

"You're a dr-drunk piece of s-shit. I s-should have l-left you years ago." My mother stutters out and then proceeds to throw gasoline on the fire that is my father's anger, by spitting blood into his face as tear tracks fall from hers. That's when it all went to hell. My dad lets out a furious roar, that I swear for a second seemed to shake the paper-thin, grimy walls of this house.

In the blink of an eye, my father throws my mother to the ground and begins to pound into her flesh without mercy.

"You"- punch - "Stupid"-punch- "Bitch"-punch.

I'm frozen in shock for a long second, wide-eyed and mouth agape, as he loses all control in his drunken fury. My mom's pained groans fill the air, making me

2

snap out of my stunned state, racing forward to stop him from killing the woman he supposedly loved once.

They weren't always like this. I remember them telling me stories from when I was little, of the time they met and fell instantly in love. Love at first sight, they said, like they knew they were meant to be together. Then I came along and it was a perfect fairy tale. But I suppose all fairy tales come with a curse, and I was that curse. The first few years were great, but then Dad started to work late, coming home drunk, and smelling of perfume that my mom didn't use. Mom started hanging out with friends, pretending she was still young and didn't have a young child at home to care for. That led to her taking drugs to forget about the fact Dad was cheating, much like herself. They ignored each other and me for the most part, but some days I wasn't invisible enough.

Mom blames me for Dad, not wanting to be home. I cried too much. I made too many messes. I didn't quite look like him enough. She never admitted it, but Dad doesn't think I'm his. My dad holds me responsible for everything that's gone wrong in his life. He blames me for my mom's drug addiction, his partying days being over, and even me not having the same hair color as them. No, I have blond hair and a rare eye coloring that is genetic. Heterochromia. So, in his mind, I'm not his child. I couldn't be.

I don't think, just act, as I ram my much smaller body into his, shoving him off her. I stumble after him, hitting the wall behind us hard. My head spins a little, but I give it a little shake to clear the feeling of being disoriented. I look over at the beaten and battered woman bleeding a mere few feet away but instantly snap my head to the right when a grunt sounds. My dad is climbing to his feet, as a monstrous sneer full of rage contorts onto his face. A chill runs down my back as fear courses through my veins and pure hatred flashes in his eyes.

"Oh, Trinity. You're just like your pathetic mother. A stupid little whore who doesn't know her place, but I'll teach you. Don't worry." He rolls his shoulders, cracking his neck side to side, reminding me of the sound of the bones I know he broke on my mom's ribs moments ago. I glance back at her for a brief moment, but all I see is blood. It's everywhere. A crime scene you would see in a horror movie, but those are fake and this is real. Her face, her body, and everything surrounding her is red. I try to see if her chest is moving, if she is breathing even just a little, but there is so much damage. I hear my dad take a step in my direction, and panic hits me like a freight train.

Run, Trinity, he is going to kill you.

I jump up to race around the kitchen table, but he is much faster. He grabs a hold of my long hair and yanks,

4

sending me flying back, landing like a heap of trash on the floor. I turned on my side to avoid the kick he tried to deliver to my prone body. I attempt to crawl away, nails digging into the floor below me, but a second booted kick collides with my side, making me slide a couple of feet, hitting the wall again. He laughs like a damned manic, enjoying my pain. The bastard. I look around for something to defend myself but only see glass from a broken picture frame that must have fallen when I hit the wall. I scoot closer, knowing it will be my last defense if I need it. My only thoughts running through my head are that I just needed to get outside, then I can run and get him and my mother help. He is just drunk out of his mind and doesn't know what he is doing right now. He will regret everything once he sleeps it off and wakes up sober tomorrow. I know it.

"Did you know your mom was a slut before you were even born? You aren't even my fucking kid, I just stuck around cuz your mom was a good fuck, doing anything I asked. She still tries to say you're mine, but I know the truth. You're weak and pathetic, nothing like me. You don't even look like me." He grins in my direction as I shake my head in denial. "Maybe I can get a good price for you over at the Lion's Den. They have some clients that like them young." He lets out a deep belly laugh this time, like selling his supposed daughter to a sleazy strip club is funny. He's a disgusting pig. How could he say all this when he helped raise me? He takes a step closer, reaching for me, ready to rid me of his life. Rage like I've never felt, lights my body on fire right before his hand makes contact with my face; All I see is red before it all goes black.

Chapter Two

Trinity

I shoot up in bed, panting hard, my heart pounding out of my chest. Instantly, my eye snaps down to my hands, but they're clean, allowing me to take a well-needed deep breath. I'm safe. It was just a nightmare, that's all. I lean back against my headboard, trying to shake the last of the dream. My sleep shorts and tank cling uncomfortably to my skin, drenched in sweat. After another minute of breathing and reassuring myself that I'm no longer dreaming, I drag myself out of bed and head straight to the bathroom.

I manage to turn the shower on to heat up and do my morning business before I finally turn to the mirror. I cringe at my appearance. Ugh, I look like a resurrected zombie. I feel it too, but it's nothing. A couple of cups of coffee can't fix. Nothing will fix the heavy-looking dark circles under my eyes, but I don't feel the need to impress anyone in this shithole town, so it doesn't matter. I finally strip out of my pajamas, stepping under the hot spray of the shower head. As I feel the tension in my shoulders melting away and the grip of my nightmares loosening, I can finally start to relax. As I shampooed, conditioned, and used my favorite cupcake-scented body wash, I mentally go through my plans for today.

It's my first day off in weeks, and I have nothing planned. I start a few online classes soon, which I'll have to fit into my schedule with working at the diner and the local newspaper, but it will be worth it. I'm giving myself one more year before I gather my belongings to head west. With the limited resources I have, the combination of both jobs, my savings, and my sheer stubbornness, I should have just enough to finally escape this place. My plan is to find a small apartment, continue my photography classes in person, and hopefully secure a new job before resorting to a diet of packaged noodles. As long as I'm far from here is all that matters.

Stepping out of the shower, I wrap a big, fluffy towel around my body, relishing in its warmth and softness, before doing the same with my hair. Looking at myself in the semi-fogged mirror, I notice a slight improvement in my appearance - I no longer look completely drained. I debate for half a second if I should apply a bit of concealer to hide the dark circles, but shrug, heading back to my room. Instead of thinking about what to do on my day off, I throw on some sweats, a sports bra, and a light jacket before heading out for an early morning run.

The outfit is simple, nothing fancy, or over the top; like some girls wear when they work out. My faded black sweats are well-loved from wear and tear over the years and my sports bar is a bit tight, but it holds these puppies in. Ignoring the small tear on the side, I slip on my light pink running jacket and get ready to go. I know my grandmother will have something to say, but she understands why I never spend money buying myself new clothes. My entire income is solely devoted to funding my escape; not a single penny goes to waste, except for essentials and maybe art supplies. Glancing over at the clock on my nightstand, I frown. It's only 5 am. *Shit.* I thought it was later. At least I got a good 5 hours of sleep today, better than most nights.

I silently creak open my bedroom door, careful to be quiet as I make my way down the hall. I know my grandma is a heavy sleeper, but I also know she will fuss over my lack of sleep again. Which I don't need right now. The old bat's stubbornness is astonishing, making it impossible for me to win an argument. She is also the one who I inherited my stubbornness from. She was a saint for taking me in at fourteen. Lord knows the first year or two, I acted out more than normal, but she understood what I had gone through and didn't blame me. Not like the rest of the town.

I stop in the kitchen, grab a glass of water, and chug it before making my way toward the entry hall. My keys, armband, headphones, and pocket knife lay in wait for me on the hallway stand. I put on my running shoes and secured my armband, ensuring that my phone is safely stored inside. The alternative rock station was already queued up, ready to set my mood. "Creep" by Radiohead fills my ears as I put in my headphones and tuck my key away. Stepping out onto the porch, I take in a deep breath. Before stepping off, heading to the back of the house that parallels the forest. The music engulfs my senses, drowning out the world around me, as I let my body effortlessly guide me to my favorite lookout point. Within minutes, my mind goes numb, and I get lost in the repetitive motion of my feet hitting compacted dirt.

I was kicking myself in the ass when I finally made it to the top of the overlook. I was so focused on expelling the last of my nightmares; It didn't occur to me to bring my camera along. As the sun appeared over the horizon, the view was truly breathtaking. The early morning light painted the sky with gentle pinks and oranges, creating a bright and vibrant scene. The sight of the deserted, sandy shores reminded me that it had been ages since I had visited the beach. It's still early October, so the mornings are chilly, with a 50/50 chance of a semi-warm midday. Today is shaping up to be one of the nicer fall days, so I'm thinking of spending my day off with a few hours at the beach followed by a painting session in the garage.

After a good 30-minute stretch, I take the trail back down toward the house I share with Gran. Making quick work as I push my muscles to their limits. I reach the back of the house in record time, my heart pounding in my chest as I struggle to catch my breath. As I walk the last few yards to the front, my eyes caught sight of a moving truck next door. I don't see anyone around, but I know the house has been up for rent for a while now. It's still early, so the rest of the neighborhood is quiet.

I head inside, knowing I'll meet whoever at some point. I casually kick off my dirty shoes to the side, feeling the cool floor beneath my bare feet. Placing my key and armband on the hall table, I head for the kitchen. A gentle hum floats towards me as I near, and I smile to myself as I pass through the doorway. In the kitchen, Gran stands by the stove, her melodious humming filling the room as she tends to her kettle of tea. To make sure I don't give the woman a heart attack, I gently clear my throat. She snaps her head up in my direction, giving me a wide smile. "Oh, good morning, sweetheart." She frowns when she fully takes me in. "Did you get any sleep last night?" With an eye roll of epic proportions, I made my way towards the coffee pot.

"Yes, I got about 5 hours before I woke up, then decided to go for a quick run to the lookout point." She eyes me with concern, but I wave her off. "I'm fine, Gran. Promise. I was thinking about heading to the beach for a few hours later today. Maybe get a few photos for my portfolio since I finally have a day off." I sigh, still feeling the exhaustion from the doubles I worked at the diner. Being short-handed this week has sucked ass, but the extra money is helpful and well needed.

"That will be nice, dear. You deserve a break. They have been working you like a damn farm horse." I giggle at that before pulling a coffee cup from the cabinet and filling it to the brim with life juice. "How you drink that black, child, I will never know." I smile widely at her while taking a big gulp, embracing the burn as it goes down.

"I like it black, just like my dark heart." I wink at her for good measure as she shakes her head and focuses back on making her own drink. Shifting the focus away from myself, I bring up what caught my attention outside a few minutes ago. "Did you see we are getting new neighbors over at the old Jacobson's place?"

She perks up at this. The woman loves any reason to bake, and baking the new neighbors a welcome to the neighborhood pie or plate of cookies will make her day. "Oh. Did you get a look at them? What do you think they would like? A cherry pie? A cake? Oh, how about a fresh batch of oatmeal chocolate chip cookies? I think I have everything for it." She shuffles around the kitchen, pulling out ingredients, placing them on the counter in an organized pile. I smile as I continue to sip my bitter coffee, savoring its robust flavor.

After a few minutes, I figure I should go get ready for my day. "Well, Gran, I'll leave you to it. I'm going to get ready to head to the beach."

She waves me off, not even bothering to look in my direction. "Yes, yes, go on. Be home for dinner. Oh, I'll have you take the cookies over later, so we can introduce ourselves." I simply hum under my breath, then head to my room. Despite being a saint, the woman maintains her belief that not all people are assholes in the end. She doesn't even know half of what I put up with in this town.

I don't bother to do more than change my clothes. Donning a pair of faded blue jeans, I feel them hug my body, revealing every curve. I hastily chose a band t-shirt, not entirely convinced it was clean, and threw on a zip-up sweatshirt to complete my look. With a swift motion, I gather my beanie, camera, sketch pad, and pen and stash them in my reliable black cross-body canvas bag. I then slide my feet into my vibrant green high-top Converse, adding a pop of color to my ensemble. I quickly gather my long blonde hair into a haphazard updo, knowing it will just become tangled, and head towards the front door. Calling out to Gran, who is in her zone as I cross the threshold of the front door, turn right, and head for the beach. As I made my way, I was enchanted by the beauty that unfolded around me. Everyone always forgets how beautiful our surroundings can be, with our eyes glued to screens all the time. I glance back at the newly rented home next door, wanting to catch a peek, but still see no one around. Shrugging, I make my way to the pier for the afternoon.

CHAPTER THREE

DANTE

We pull up to our newly rented home in the small town of Tall Pines, Maine. I hate taking jobs so far from home, but this was necessary for us. The guy we are hunting has gotten away with a few things one too many times. Pissing off our boss for the last time. Now, we have the job of cleaning up the mess.

I peer over at the four-bedroom, two-bath home in front of us. It's one of those all-American-looking ones. Where a family with a loving husband and wife with two kids and a dog should be living. Not the three of us. The house is painted a soft blue color with white trim. I already feel so improper here. We are going to stand out like a sore thumb with our less-than-all-American looks.

The guys and I scream danger with our tattoos, piercings, and black leather jackets. Furthest from a Ken doll as possible. Lucky for us, this job is only for a month. Observe, report, and then wait for instructions. Easy, really, so might as well treat it like a mini vacation.

"August, check the house. Chase, grab the bags. I'll let the boss man know we arrived." They both nod before heading off. Pulling out my phone, I notice it's 6 a.m. here, which means it's 3 a.m. back home. Damn. I pull up the secure email we use and send our response.

To: Boss Man
From: Heathens
Made it. Will check in again when we have more to report.

Sweet and simple. Just the way we like it. I hit send, pocketing my phone, and followed the guys inside. Entering the house, I see an open-plan living room and kitchen. A hallway to the right leads to what I'm guessing are back rooms. I see August coming from that direction. "All secured." He calls out before heading to the kitchen, groaning when he sees the cabinets and fridge empty.

"Hey fuckers, why don't you come help carry your shit? What the fuck did you even pack, D? Your bag weighs as much as a ton of bricks." He grimaces, squeezing through the door frame, carrying an arm full of bags, dropping them in the middle of the room.

"Careful. I brought some reading material and would prefer not to have to kill you for ruining them." I glare at him as he just shrugs.

"Dude, they make porn in video form now. No need to carry around your dirty magazines everywhere." I roll my eyes at his antics and ignore his stupidity. From the kitchen, August let out a loud snort that echoed through the empty house.

"Idiots. Let's bring in the rest of the furniture and shit. Then August can go do the food shopping while Chase and I start recon." I look over at idiot number one. "Can you get eyes on the subject? I'll check out the town and get the lay of the land."

"Aye aye, captain." He gives me a two-finger salute, making me shake my head in annoyance, a headache already forming. It's too early to put up with his shit right now.

"You know, if I didn't call you assholes, my brothers. I would have killed you already." August snorts again while Chase bats his lashes, placing a folded hand under his chin.

"You say the nicest things to us. I knew you loved me." He winks, blowing me a kiss, but when I take a step towards him to possibly knock him out, he rushes back outside, cackling like the manic he is. I look up at the ceiling and pray to anyone listening to give me patience with these guys.

Unpacking the moving van went by pretty quickly, but it's still noon by the time we finished putting things in their place. We had little other than simple personal items like my books, August's art and paint supplies, and Chase's weight equipment. We made a fairly large order to get the bigger furniture we might need for the living room and bedrooms delivered in a few days. With all that settled, we head out to do recon.

August hops in the van to head to the store for food and essentials for the house. He'll switch cars as well. Chase hops on his bike to hunt down our target to start tracking his movements. I headed out towards the beach we saw coming in. I need a moment to decompress from the trip. This entire year has been job after job with no actual breaks other than the off chance we get to go somewhere fun, but that's few and far between. Every few weeks, the boss orders us to a new city, a new state, and a new target, all in the name of business. It's exhausting and, for once, I just want a chance to relax and not have to worry about the next poor fucker that crosses the boss man.

It took me roughly 20 minutes to get to the beach, but it was worth the walk. The combination of the sun's glistening rays on the water and the rhythmic crashing of the waves is nothing short of breathtaking. I head further down the shoreline to the pier area, spotting a few locals here and there. No one really pays much attention to me, which is a good thing in my line of work.

When I finally reach the pier, I notice a tiny figure at the end lying on the ground, almost lifeless. I'm a bit confused about what is going on, but when I hear a groan, I rush forward. Concern flooding my system. What if it's a child who is injured or lost? Children have always been my weakness; I can't stand someone taking advantage of an innocent soul not yet corrupted by the world. As I get closer, the small figure must hear my approach, making them jerk up, banging their head on the railing that skirts the edge of the old wooden pier.

"Mother-fucking son of a donkey's ass."

I pull up short as the cussing gets louder; the figure climbing to their feet, turning to glare daggers at me. And holy shit. I'm pretty sure my jaw just hit the floor.

"Who the fuck are you and why the hell are you running up on me like that?" She pulls the black beanie she was wearing off her head, making a tangle of golden blonde hair tumble down her back. She rubs at her head a bit more, but I'm speechless. The woman is a fucking goddess. I slowly soak in the round, thick curve of her body in a pair of faded jeans and a plain zip-up hoodie. With her feet clad in vivid, bright green high-top shoes, the little thing stood before me, barely reaching my chest. She is like the perfect pint-size fire-cracker of rage right now, and I mean rage. "Well, are you going to answer me or just stand there, asshole?" My eyes snap back up to her face, widening as I take in this work of art. I notice the breathtaking woman has two very different colored eyes. One is a bright forest green while the other an electric blue, both are full of annoyance. She huffs, leaning down, grabs a bag I didn't notice and turns to leave. Shit. No. She can't leave yet.

"Wait," I call out, making her pause. She peers over her shoulder, cocking a brow in a *what the hell do you want* look. "I'm sorry. I, umm, I saw you from the end of the pier lying on the ground and thought you were an injured kid or something. I didn't mean to scare you, making you hit your head."

"Is that supposed to be some kind of short girl joke or something?" She questions and I swear I start to panic.

"What? No. I meant from afar you seemed small, not like a kid, but kinda like a kid. Shit, this isn't coming out right. Can I start over?" I ask, hoping she pities me enough to say yes. She stares at me for a moment, doing her own once over. She must see something she likes, because she finally rolls her eyes.

"Sure." I let out a breath I didn't know I was holding. *Who the fuck is this woman?* I've never been this awkward talking to the female species before in my life. Shit, not to be an asshole, but I rarely have to talk to them to get them bent over something with my dick buried in them.

"Hi. I'm Dante." I say, almost face-palming myself. She smirks over at me before biting her lip. That simple move sent a bolt of lust straight to my already semi-hard cock.

"Well, Dante. I'm in a good mood today, so it's your lucky day. I could use your assistance. Mind helping a girl out?" She asks before I see her eyes slide down my body. I see exactly when her eyes land on my crotch, because her eyes widen for half a second before going half-mass with desire. "Yeah, I think you can help me out just fine." She nods to follow her, and I hesitate for half a second before she turns away and starts walking backwards. "Well? Are you going to apologize to me or not?" Yes, yes, I am. I'll apologize in a thorough and extensive manner, ensuring my sincerity to the fullest.

CHAPTER FOUR

TRINITY

H *oly shit, am I really doing this? I think I am. I'm about to do this.*

When I came out here today, I wasn't expecting to slam my head into the railing of the pier when I heard pounding footsteps coming up fast behind me. Then I definitely didn't expect a huge, tattooed, sexy-as-sin asshole being the one scaring my half to death. I peek behind me once more, as I lead Dante to the beach house down the way. Despite the broken lock, it has gained a reputation as a hidden spot for lovers to rendezvous. While also doubling as a storage space for a hodgepodge of beach toys and life vests for children. Dante follows behind like an obedient puppy, making me smile. Men are idiots, I swear. They might have two heads, but only ever think with one.

I give him a quick appraisal, noting his attire and any handsome features. He doesn't seem familiar, especially with his bad boy appearance, so I assume he is just passing through town and wanted to see the ocean. Perfect for me. I can hit it and quit it with the best of them. Sex is always better when you don't have to deal with emotions afterwards. It's like a transaction; we both get something out of it.

Dante screams my type, all bad boy and rough around the edges. I wonder if he will fuck me hard and dirty, since that's all I really want right now. The sight of his tattoos, stretching across his neck and wrists, make me think he might be one large piece of artwork as my fingers twitch to trace the lines.

"How old are you, Cupcake?" *Cupcake? Really.* Men and their ridiculous pet names for women.

"Almost 21 and you?" I know the man is older than me, but might as well know how old. Dante has dark black hair that is shaved short on the sides and longer on top. With a jawline that could cut glass, his steel-gray eyes were impossible to ignore. Especially when accentuated by lashes that were thick and envy-inducing. He is over 6 feet, much taller than me; which isn't saying much since I'm as short as a fucking oompaloompa, but without the orange skin. Dante's skin is sun-kissed, so I'm guessing he is one of those guys who walks around shirtless all summer. He has completed the typical bad boy look with black jeans, a dark tee, a leather jacket, and black work boots.

"23. So what were you doing laying on the pier?" He asks, still just trailing behind me. *What if I was planning on killing him?* He would never be the wiser, since his dick is doing all the thinking.

"Taking photos. What were you doing running up to a lone woman like that? What if I thought you were some crazy serial killer trying to kidnap me and I tried to stab you?" I peer over my shoulder again when I hear him snort, but don't bother commenting how I really could have stabbed him with my pocket knife. We arrived at our destination as I swung open the door to the beach house, Dante following right behind, stepping into my space. I shiver as his chest molds to my back as he leans down to run his nose up my neck. Of course, I tilt my head, giving him better access and making me scream at my traitorous pussy. *What a fucking hussy.* We haven't gotten laid in weeks. Months? *Fuck, when was the last time I had a good fuck?*

I don't have time to think about it because the next moment, teeth nip at my earlobe before his husky sexual voice fills my ears. "Maybe I like a bit of rough foreplay before I make you see stars." God. I'm so fucked up.

Am I seriously about to fuck a stranger in a beach house, who I think just admitted he wouldn't have minded if I stabbed him? Yes! Yes, the fuck I am.

I spin in his hold, whipping out said pocket knife, flipping it open, and placing it at the crease of his neck. Smiling wide when I hear him let out a soft, low groan. So potentially he could be a serial killer. "Look, since we will never see each other again, let's make this quick and dirty. I have somewhere I need to be." He gives me a wicked smirk before stepping even closer into my space. The blade digs in where I still hold the knife until he lets out a small hiss of pain when it finally splits the skin. It's barely a paper cut, but I need to hurry this along. Gran will be making a shit ton of cookies that I'll have to deliver to our new neighbors soon.

"Quick and dirty is my specialty, but I have to ask." I cock a brow at his words. Despite the dimming light in the small room, I could still make out his strong facial features. Like how his eyes roll back for a second when he takes a deep inhale. "Do you taste as good as you smell, Cupcake?" I've never been so grateful for my favorite body wash until now. This time I pull the knife away, folding in the blade and returning it to my jacket pocket as I step into his space. Our bodies are now pressed against each other, chest to chest. His body warmth instantly envelops me, and I can't resist breathing in his masculine scent. I moan as the smell of worn leather and something like old books fills my senses.

I stand on my tippy-toes, placing my lips on his collarbone before nipping at the skin. Dante lets out another soft groan, the sound making a heat coil in my core. I lift higher till my lips meet the edge of his ear before I whisper, "Why don't you find out?" Then I bite his ear, hard. Dante growls, gripping my hips, lifting me into the air. I automatically wrap my legs around his hips, feeling what the man is working with. *Oh, god. Is he even a man?* He feels huge, and he isn't even undressed.

He shuffles over to an old plastic beach chair and all but tosses me down. My ass hits the chair before bouncing. I let out a small shriek, prepared to feel the pain of hitting the hard ground, but Dante is there, pushing my hips into the fabric. He leers over me like a wolf who just cornered its little bunny prey, and a thrill of excitement zaps through my body. *Fuck.* Dante's steel-gray eyes are now full-blown, covered with lust as they glance down at my still-clothed body. He softly hums under his breath before his next words give me pause. "Just remember you asked for this. I'm going to have a taste of that sweet little pussy of yours before I give you what you really want. Quick and dirty Cupcake and you will scream for me."

Before I can even comprehend what is happening next, my jeans are being ripped down my legs, taking my underwear with them. My ankles are now locked together by my jeans and shoes still on. Dante spreads my thighs wide before ducking under my legs and diving right in. *Oh, holy hell.* He acts as if he has been starving for days, and only my juices can quench his thirst. His tongue laps at my core in long, hard licks, and I can't do anything but thrash in his powerful hold. If I didn't know any better, I would say this was his day job. It's as if his tongue was made specifically for pleasure because it feels as if everything happens within seconds. My back arches off the beach chair, my toes curl, and I damn near scream the roof off as my orgasm hits me like a tsunami. The asshole doesn't stop as he sucks on my clit, drinking up my juices like a fine wine. After another minute of blissful aftershocks, my body relaxes. Dante pops his head up between my legs, grinning like a damn psychopath. "I can confirm you taste as yummy as the cupcakes you smell like." A laugh burst out of me; I couldn't help it. His words, combined with the lust still blanketing his features, are just plain sinful and ridiculous. Guys like him don't go for girls like me.

"Fuckkkk... you have the tongue of the devil; I think I'll call you Lucifer." He chuckles at that before removing himself from between my thick thighs. I go to sit up, but Dante grips my hips.

"Where do you think you're going?" He looks down at my exposed core and licks his lips like a dog getting a treat. "That was just an appetizer. I'm ready for the main course. Now be a good girl and scream for me." Before I can give him a piece of my mind and tell him I scream for no one, I'm being flipped around. Hands-on my hips as he yanks me up and back, forcing me to my hands and knees. The sound of a belt clinking, the rustling of fabric dropping. A second later, Lucifer is thrusting into me and, as he told me to do, I scream. The sensation of being filled in a single rough thrust causes my pussy to clamp down tight around Dante's length. I knew the man felt fucking big, but fuck, he feels monstrous inside me. He is thick and long and is hitting all the right spots. I realize he hasn't moved in a long minute, but I can feel him towering over me, allowing me to adjust to his immense size. *I guess chivalry is not dead after all.*

The moment I relax, he senses it and begins to move. Slow at first; painfully slow and after his first few thrusts, something cold and foreign rubs against my inner walls. *Holy shit. Is Lucifer pierced?* I don't have time to process that fact because Dante leans forward, gripping my shoulders tight, then slams me back on his cock like he is trying to turn me into a shish-kabob. A moan builds in my throat as he fucks me hard and rough, using me like a rag doll as his hips slap against my ass.

Another thrust, and another moan escapes on a gasp of breath. A second later, a firm palm lands on my ass, causing me to jerk forward. I don't get far as Dante slams me back against his monster cock, causing me to scream in pain and pleasure. Lucifer grunts behind me, his movement becoming jerky. *Oh, he is close.* I tighten my walls, hearing him release another groan at the sensation; a second later he leans over me to reach under my chest, finding a tight pebbled nipple, then pinches it hard. Sending my body into another euphoric, out-of-the-blue orgasm. Lucifer follows me over the edge a second later, thrusting deep into me one last time. A thin layer of sweat coats our skin, causing goosebumps to travel up my body as he lifts himself. My body still feels like jello as I lay there, face down, as the sound of Lucifer dressing again fills the small room.

A phone goes, causing me to jump before Dante speaks. "Yeah. I'm on my way back now." He pauses, making me look back up at him. His eyes trail down my body as he smirks with male satisfaction. "Yeah, I'm here. Sorry. I got caught up with the view. See you soon." He hangs up, pocketing his phone. I finally find the strength to roll over, wiggling my underwear and jeans back up over my hips. "Well, Cupcake. It's been great, but I gotta head out." He fishes out his wallet before grabbing two twenties, handing them over to me. Rage like none other begins to boil my blood.

Did he think I was some kind of hooker? Forty bucks for a good fuck. I think I will stab the fucker.

When I don't take the money, he frowns down at me. "Look Cupcake." That name is going to get him killed faster. "I didn't use a rubber. The money is for the pill. I ain't ready to be a baby daddy, and I doubt we will see each other again. So unless you wanna raise a mini Heathen on your own, take the money." His words finally reached my rage-filled brain. No rubber.

"You didn't use a fucking condom!" I growl, glaring at the big fucker like I don't come up to his chest in size. The asshole shrugs.

"After tasting your sweet pussy, I couldn't wait to have you wrapped around me. I'm clean, if that's what you're worried about?" He frowns again before tilting his head. "Should I be worried?" The nerve of this fucker. I don't bother replying. I grin wide before throwing my fist straight at his face. His eyes widen, but he is either too shocked or just plain slow to stop my knuckles from colliding with his nose. The crunch of bone fills my ears as he howls at the sudden pain. Not wasting any more time with the asshole, I snatch my bag plus the forty bucks that he dropped and head for the door. When I get to the doorway, I call out, "Thanks for the good fuck, Lucifer."

CHAPTER FIVE

TRINITY

As I make my way home; I curse myself, feeling the pain in my swollen knuckles from punching the asshole's stupid face, and knowing that Gran is going to have words about it. Do I tell Gran I fucked a stranger in the beach house, then punched him in the face after he tried to hand me money and asked if I was clean? No. The woman would have a heart attack on the spot, roll over in her grave, and then come back as a ghost just to lecture me about my poor choices in life. *Yeah, I'm not telling Gran shit.* I'll say I tripped and fell.

Once home, I stomp my way to the kitchen, the smell of freshly baked cookies assaulting my nose as I head straight to the freezer. Gran gives me a bewildered look before rushing forward. "Trinity, sweetheart, what happened? Are you okay?" She reaches for my hand, but I cover it with a bag of frozen peas.

"I'm fine, Gran. I tripped and fell on the pier trying to get a better landscape shot." She eyes my injured hand for a long minute, probably debating whether I'm lying to her. She must either believe me or decide it's not worth the lecture. Either way, I'm grateful for a chance to change the topic.

"You know what would make me feel better?" I ask, eyeing the large plate of cookies cooling on the counter. She looks in said direction and scoffs, the sound echoing through the air. She actually scoffs at me.

"You know those are for the new neighbors, but..." she pauses, eyeing my hand. "If you tell me the truth about what happened to your hand, I'll let you have one." She grins widely at the scowl now mirroring my face.

"On second thought, I believe I will go shower. It's been a long day." I turn to head for my room, but Gran's voice stops me before I can escape.

"Dress in something nice, sweetheart. I want to invite the new neighbors for a nice little dinner. From what I saw earlier, I think there is at least one gentleman your age." I peer over my shoulder, cocking a brow in question. "Oh yes, he looked very handsome... and fit." I can practically see hearts in her eyes from here. The woman has tried to set me up on more blind dates than I care to admit. If I didn't know better, I would think the woman was hoping for a few grand babies soon. The thought of me having kids instantly puts me in a bad mood, reminding me of Lucifer and his magic fucking tongue. How dare he assume I was just going to allow myself to end up pregnant with some randos kid? It's a cruel world out here for women, and the moment I was old enough, I made sure I was on birth control. For several reasons, one being not all guys take no for an answer and won't bother to wrap themselves up in the force of the moment.

What was I even thinking, not making him rubber up like that? Oh yeah, that devil tongue of his was sinful on my pussy, and I could have agreed to just about anything as long as he stayed between my legs. *Damn, my weakness for a good rough and dirty fuck.*

When I reach my room, I kick my door shut behind me, turning to look at myself in the standing mirror attached to the back of the door. *Well, shit.* No wonder Gran eyed me so suspiciously. I looked well fucked, with my golden blonde hair a mess and a smudge of dirt on my right cheek where I was pushed into the beach chair. Sandy spots covering parts of my clothes. Oh well, It's not like I'll have to see Lucifer ever again. From what I overheard, the asshole was just making a pit stop to stretch his legs. *Good riddance.*

After my second shower of the day, I feel more relaxed. Maybe I have time to head to the garage and get some painting done. I glance at the clock, seeing that it's 4 p.m. *Shit.* Gran will probably want to have dinner around six, so if I want any time to myself, I better hurry.

I dress in another pair of faded jeans, this time black, and throw on a black tank top with a sheer black top to go over it. Nice and cute, the way Gran would want me to look. Quickly, applying a thin layer of black kohl under my eyes, a quick swipe of mascara to my lashes, my cupcake ChapStick, and I'm good to go. I don't bother with my hair after towel drying it; I just let it do its thing and hope for the best. To finish out my look, I add my red high tops for a pop of color, and head downstairs.

This time I find Gran in the living room watching her favorite crime show. The woman is obsessed with all things Criminal Minds. I swear, she might actually want to be a professional serial killer if she were younger and could haul a dead body around. When she finally notices me, she gives me a once-over before honest to god rolling her eyes. "I suppose that will do. I wish you would cover up those tattoos. You'll never find a husband if you don't start acting like a lady." I snort, very unlady like I might add.

"Gran, he isn't the man for me if he can't accept me and all my flaws." She just hums under her breath before getting up and heading to the kitchen. I walk behind, fully aware that she is about to force me to engage with people.

"Now take these next door and invite the family over for a nice dinner." She pauses to think. "How about a roast? No. Meatloaf. Or maybe spaghetti. Everyone likes spaghetti, right?" I shrug, not knowing how to answer. I love food in general. Anyone can tell from my hips. "Perhaps you should ask if anyone has any allergies."

"Gran. You don't even know if they will want to come over. I'm sure they have been moving and unpacking all day. They are probably tired. The cookies are enough." Plus, I've done enough peopling today, and I'm not sure if I have the mental capacity to deal with more strangers.

"I suppose, but I still want you to offer. I bet after moving all day, whoever lives, there will be hungry and too tired to cook. It doesn't hurt to ask. Now go on." I let out an exasperated sigh, but smile when Gran holds up a single cookie, waving it in the air to catch my attention. "I saved this one for you, sweetheart. Now go on and finish it before you speak to them. No one wants to see you chewing food." I roll my eyes but smile wide when I take my first bite of the delicious goodness.

Without further instruction or encouragement, I head for the front door, munching on my oatmeal chocolate chip cookie and hoping our new neighbors aren't jerks. I really don't want to punch another person for not accepting a little old lady's dinner invitation.

CHAPTER SIX

AUGUST

My trip into town was pretty uneventful. I stopped at a few shops to grab the essentials like basic cleaning supplies, food for the house, bathroom and washing items, and more. I found a small, tucked away art supply shop that I had to check out. I grabbed a new set of charcoal pencils and some new colors of acrylic paint that I don't have yet. After checking out at the grocery store, I went home to check in with the guys. I'm the first one home, so I go about unpacking everything and putting things away.

I'm midway through setting up a canvas to start a new project when the front door bangs open. I tense for a second, ready to make a move if needed, but Chase's voice rings through the air in the next second. "Honey. I'm home. Where's my dinner?" I roll my eyes at the idiot. I love the man like a brother, but I swear if we didn't live together regularly, I would probably kill him. Or at least cut out his tongue.

"In my room," I call out to let him know I'm also home. I hear thundering footsteps following my response and pound through the house until a shadow is cast in the doorway. "How was your job?" I ask knowing he had to establish eyes on our target and watch his movement for a few hours.

"Boriiinnnggggg. Why do I always get the lame jobs?" I snort at that. Nothing is lame about our jobs. Some might be less exciting than others, but never lame. "Where's D?" He questions like he just realized the last member of our crew is missing.

I shrug. "No idea. Wanna call and check on him?" I continue to set up my paint station as I watch from the corner of my eye as he pulls out his phone and dials Dante. It takes a few rings until Chase speaks.

"D. What's your ETA? I'm hungry and August won't feed me." He whines like a child, making me roll my eyes. I swear, Chase is like that little brother you wish you never had but would fuck someone up if they messed with him. It's like the "I'm the only one that can beat him up" kind of brotherly love. Not that any of us are blood brothers, but we learned a long time ago blood doesn't make you family, the bond you share does. And the guys and I have bonded over our shit lives, making us stronger together.

They share a few more words that I miss before Chase pockets his phone and stares at me with his big blue puppy dog eyes. "Dude. Where is D?" I ask, ignoring his sad eyes as I finish my setup.

"He is on his way. He said he got caught up with the view. Whatever that means?" I frown at that. Dante isn't one to get distracted by views. Shit, we have been all over the world and seen some fantastic views, so I doubt anything here would catch his attention.

"Soooooo... What's for dinner? Because I'm starving. I bet I could eat a whole cow by myself." I continue to ignore him as I head to the kitchen. "Look at me, Aug." From the corner of my eye, I see him lift his shirt. "I'm wasting away. I need food ASAP." I open the cupboard, grab a bag of trail mix and toss it at his face. He catches it, of course, and wastes no time ripping open the bag and shoveling a handful into his mouth.

"We can decide on dinner when Dante gets home. I saw a diner in town where we could grab food. It's been a long day and I don't feel like cooking."

It took Dante 20 minutes to return home from our call, and I was astonished to see him arrive with blood running down his nose and over his lip, with a few drops staining his shirt. "What the fuck happened to you?" I ask, grabbing one of the new washcloths and wetting it before heading towards him to see the damage.

"Long story." He grumbles, taking the washcloth from me and pressing it against his face. Chase walks into the room a second later, pausing in the middle of the living room, glancing back and forth between me and Dante. He narrows his eyes at Dante before speaking.

"Did you get a nose job, D?" D lunges at Chase as he breaks out in over-the-top laughter. Chase grabs at his stomach, tears running down his face as he cackles at his comment. D took the moment to tackle Chase to the ground, raising a fist and throwing it into Chase's side. I heave out a deep exhale. I live with animals.

"Enough you too!" They both pause, looking up at me. I cross my arm over my chest and glare at the idiots. Chase smiles up at me with a shit-eating grin, while Dante just scowls. "Dante, tell us what happened? And most importantly, is there a body we need to take care of?" I ask, realizing blood means a clean-up job. I hate clean-up jobs.

"Nobody. She walked away before I could bend her over my knee and spank her." I pause at his words. She? Her? What?

Chase must have caught on at the same time, as he jumped up off the floor and smirked at D. "You let a girl beat you up? Was it a Girl Scout because those little girls are vicious? I tried to buy a box of shortbread cookies one time, but the little brat had just sold the last box, so I told her she was rude. So, she kicked me in the shin and that fucking hurt, dude. Those little girls are just plain mean." He winces as if he was remembering the pain of the kick he most definitely deserved.

"No. It wasn't a fucking Girl Scout it was a little pint size ball of fury." He smiled to himself and I narrow my eyes. He sees my look and sighs, shoulders sagging as he heads to the kitchen to rinse the washcloth out. "I was getting the lay of the land. So, I walked down to the beach we saw on the way in. When I got to the pier, I saw a slight form on the ground, so I went to check it out, thinking someone has hurt a kid or someone. Well, it wasn't." He sighs again. "It was a chick who was taking photos of the landscape or something. Anyway, I scared her and she hit her head. She must have hit her head extra hard because she led me to a little beat-up shack."

"So she kicked your ass for scaring her?" Chase asks, eyeing him with a goofy grin.

"No, she wanted a good fucking with a bad boy with a nice cock. She mentioned never seeing me again, so I think she was just passing through, anyway. But fuck, man, you should have seen her. She was a fucking goddess with the most intense eyes. One was a bright crystal blue and the other an earthly emerald green."

"Damn, dude. Writing poetry now. Did you get her name and number? Maybe you can meet up again and introduce me." Chase wags his eyebrows up and down in the perv kinda way.

"Dude, I doubt it ended well since D came home with a busted face," I say, glancing back at said face. It doesn't look broken, but she got him good.

"Maybe his cock isn't as good as he thought. Perhaps she just needs a real man to fuck her senseless." Chase replies, this time flexing his arms as if saying having muscles makes him a real man. Dante growls before launching himself at Chase again, making me have to step between them to halt his advance.

"Continue. What happened, for you to get a busted face?" I wave my hand in continuous motion.

"I ate her out first and fuckkkk, she tasted so fucking good, sweet like sugar. Then I flipped her around and slammed into her. It was like coming home for the first time in months. Anyways, I fucked her hard and quick, as she asked for. We both knew this was a one-time, never seeing each other, and both got off kinda fuck. So, I got dressed, then you called." He nods to Chase. "Anyways, I handed her forty bucks to get the pill since I don't need no chick. I don't know, having my spawn. I told her we don't need no little Heathens running around. Then I asked if I should be worried about catching anything." He winces at that. I almost want to punch him in the face, too.

"You actually asked her that after you fucked her raw?" Chase asks, looking shocked himself. D shrugs in answer. "No wonder you got punched in the face. Shit, I'm not even that much of an asshole, dude. You never answered if you got her name and number. Maybe you should apologize?" Dante shakes his head.

"No, but fuck, I think I let the love of my life walk away, and I'll never see her again." I cock a brow at that. "She was perfect. Tight and sexy body. Sexual voice. Sweet tasting pussy and man, can she throw a punch." We all stand there for a second before Chase and I start laughing. Go figure. Dante meets his match, then goes and fucks it all up.

Dante grumbles to himself before tossing the now pinkish cloth in the sink. "I'm going to go shower. Then we can go find food. I worked up an appetite." He smirks to himself before heading down the hall that leads to the bathroom. I'm about to head back to my room when the sound of knocking echoes off the empty living room. I frown at Chase, who just shrugs before heading to the kitchen, probably to find more snacks. I'm the only mature adult in this damn group.

I head for the front door when another round of knocking can be heard. I swing open the door, ready

51

to scowl and berate our impatient visitor, but I freeze. "Oh, umm, can I help you?"

The blonde-haired beauty snaps her head up from staring at a covered plate in her hands. "No. Yes. I meannnn... Hi. I'm Trinity and I live next door with my Gran. She made you cookies." She thrusts the plate into my chest, shaking me out of the mildly stunned state I was in. "Oh, she would like you and your family to come over for dinner. How about an hour? Sound good?" She asks and I just nod. "Do you speak?" she asks, eyeing me from head to toe. She pauses at my waist area and I pray she can't see my dick imprint because I've never gotten hard so fast in my life. The tiny bombshell beauty bites her lip, making me groan, but that is not what startles me.

Chase walks up behind me, clapping me on the back. "Dude, who is at the.... Holy shit! Where have you been all my life and can I get your number?" She barks out a laugh before rolling her eyes, apparently immune to Chase's wicked good looks and charm.

"Not happening, Lover boy. Anyways..." She turns back to me, giving me her full,   and my eyes widen in shock. No. That can't be. "Look, I can see this is a bachelor pad now, but Gran doesn't get to socialize much anymore, so be a gentleman and come to dinner. Plus, you get a free meal. What's to lose?" I nod my head like a fucking bobble head because what else can I say? "Good. So how many are there? Just you two?"

"Ummm. No. Three." Wow, I stared like a dumbass but didn't D say the girl he met had two different colored eyes and his words were "a little pint size ball of fury". Shit, what will happen if these two meet again? Last time she punched him in the nose, what will happen next?

"Yeah, our brother is in the shower, we will be there soon. What do I get if I'm a good boy?" Chase waggles his brows in a sexual gesture, and I elbow him in the ribs. Luckily, he is basically an overgrown golden retriever. "Oh cookies. I love cookies." He snatches the plate before turning and heads back to the kitchen. Trinity stares after him with a cocked brow.

"Okay. So, one hour and best behavior for Gran. Got it?"

"Yeah. Best behavior, got it." She beams up at me, nods, then turns on her heel, calling over her shoulder as she goes.

"Great, see you then. Oh, and Gran is making spaghetti, and she cooks for an army, so bring your appetite."

Oh, I'll bring my appetite alright, but it won't be for the pasta.

I close the door as my mind wanders back to her eyes. Maybe heterochromia isn't as common as you think, but I know that Trinity is the woman Dante fucked, insulted, and fell in love with after she punched him in the face. Well, Chase thought this job was going to be boring, but I think it just got that much more interesting.

Oh, Trinity, you have no idea the Heathens you just invited over. I smile at that thought. Oh yes, this month is going to be fun.

CHAPTER SEVEN

TRINITY

W hat the hell is wrong with me? Could I be any more awkward? Yes, but did the new neighbors need to be so fucking hot? I just got fucked by a hot asshole in a beat-up beach house, and now my pussy is ready for another pounding. And they are brothers! The image of three sets of hands caressing my body pops into my head. Fuck. Nope. We are not going there.

I head back through my front gate and up the front steps into the house. The moment Gran hears me enter, she calls out. "Trinity, what did they say? Will they be coming over? Any allergies?" I don't answer right away but head in her direction towards the kitchen. The woman is fluttering around the kitchen, grabbing items from the fridge and cupboards, laying things out, and preparing for the feast I know she will make. Gran loves to bake and cook. Feeding people has always been a passion of hers. I'm not even sure how I'm not

300 pounds by now with how much she overcooks. Of course, I have a healthy appetite, but the woman always makes more than needed for the two people living under this roof. I watch as she pulls fresh tomatoes and herbs for the pasta sauce. She also has everything to make her homemade pasta noodles and the best garlic bread known to mankind. I think in another life, Gran was a 5-star chef or something. When I've taken too long to answer, she pauses in her frantic motions and looks at me expectantly.

"Yes, Gran, you will have dinner guests to fawn over your cooking tonight." She smiles excitedly, like a puppy who just got their first ball thrown for them. She turns back around and starts turning on and measuring out items. "By the way, it's three grown men, so I doubt you'll have leftovers."

"Oh perfect. Were they handsome?" she asks, glancing back like she is thinking about planning a wedding and great-grandbabies. Before she can start in on me, I abruptly turn and book it to the garage, her laughter following in my wake.

Entering the garage gives me the chance to fully breathe. The scent of paint and my photo development chemicals fill my nose. It's not the greatest scent, but it calms me. This is my space, my place to decompress and just be me. To express myself to the fullest.

Flipping the switch, the lights flicker a moment before bright light assaults my eyes. I head straight for my new blank canvas set up across the room. I have pictures from today that I need to develop, but that would take longer than the hour that I have before I subject myself to people. Sexy people, but still people.

I grab out my brushes and paint, staring at the canvas for a minute to decide what new project I want to start. An image flashes in my mind and I groan. Ugh. I try to picture anything else to do but when my mind seems adamant about the image; I relent. I pull out my phone, finding my music app before hitting shuffle. "Dancing in a Daydream" by Roses and Revolutions comes through the Bluetooth speaker I have connected in here. Turning back to my blank canvas, I close my eyes and picture him. The way he gazes up at me from between my legs. Like a man starved of a woman's touch. I decided to paint that exact moment. I start to gather the paints I will need as I sway to the music, and my mind begins to replay that scene over and over like a pornography movie stuck on repeat.

I start with my thighs, covering both the right and left of the large piece. I do a rough outline to get my portions right before I start in on Dante's face. I focus on his eyes after I framed a rough outline of his face at my apex. I figured I'd start at the center of the piece and work my way to the outside before going to clean up lines and add small details. I know it won't be perfect, but it's clear that it's him if he were to ever see it. Not that he would. I'll probably burn the canvas and piece after. It's kinda like that saying guys use... Fuck them to get them out of your system. Well, I'll paint him to get him out of mine.

His eyes are the most expressive. The steel-gray coloring felt like he glowed with a wild hunger when he stared up at me. It felt like he had waited his whole life to be in that exact spot at that exact time. He worshiped my pussy like his life depended on it. *Fuck, fuck, fuck. Stop thinking about that asshole Trinity.* The devil was said to be a sinfully good-looking man until you sold your soul to him, and he burned you alive in the pits of hell. And I know for a fact that man was fucking Lucifer, the devil himself.

I focus back on my piece as a whole with what I saw and not felt, once again losing myself in my work and the music as it reverberated around the room, filling my soul with tranquility.

I must have been completely lost in my work again because I practically jump out of my skin as a vaguely familiar deep voice sounds from behind me. "Holy shit, that's beautiful." I spin around in a blur, glaring at the newcomer who dared enter my peaceful sanctuary. I glare at the man who answered the door earlier, realizing I never got his name. He ignores my death stare, stepping forward to get a better look at the piece I was lost in. Before I can tell the fucker to get the fuck out, he surprises me. "I love the line work. It reminds me of Laura Lee Zanghetti, but more sexual. It's breathtaking really. I can feel the emotion in his eyes, the lust, like he is worshiping this woman." Well, shit. I didn't think a man talking about my art that no one ever saw would be such a turn-on.

"First off, you know who Laura Lee Zanghetti is? And second, who are you?" I place my brush down on the table next to my palette and turn down the music. I stare at him expectantly, cross my arms over my chest, popping my hip and a second away from tapping my foot in annoyance.

"Yes. I know who she is, and we met like an hour ago. I'm your new neighbor." He eyes me with a frown, making me roll my eyes.

"I know that, but you never actually introduced yourself," I say, making his eyes widen before he reaches up, rubbing the back of his neck as pink tints his cheek. Is he embarrassed? How cute. I take a second to fully take the man in. He's tall, at least 6 '2' or 6'3', but that's not saying much when I'm a whopping 5 foot. He's wearing a nice gray button-up shirt, the top two buttons undone, showing dark lines of artwork. Of course, he had to roll the sleeve up his forearm, in that way that melts women's panties all over the world. Tattoos line his arms, tracing under his sleeves as well. His pants are deep navy-blue jeans, fitted to shape his muscular thighs and firm ass. It should be a crime for a man to have a nicer ass than a woman. It's actually just plain rude.

I focus back on his face. His hair falls to his ear and looks like it might cover his eyes often. It also looks super soft, giving me the urge to want to run my hand through it. He has stronger features but is not rough or scary-looking. His eyes are a pretty forest green color that seems to swirl with an edge of gold.

"Shit. I'm sorry, I'm August." He sticks out his hand for me to shake. I go to reach in, since Gran taught me manners when I notice something. I grip his hand but don't shake. I bring it closer to my face and just as I thought.

"You paint too?" I ask, looking at his brightly colored stained fingers. Sometimes, all the soap and scrubbing in the world can't remove all the paint. His hands were currently covered in blues, browns, and whites. "You were painting the beach, weren't you?"

"How di-" He shakes his head. "I guess it takes one to know one." I grin at that. "And yes. I have had no real inspiration lately, but scenery is usually a safe bet." He blushes again, and I find that really cute. We stand there for another second before a knock comes from the door leading into the house. That's Gran's cue to come in.

"Well Picasso, Gran has been waiting to cook for guests for a while, and I'm sure it's all ready to go." He nods.

"I was actually supposed to come get you. She told me to knock, and I did, but when you didn't answer, I came in, then saw what you were working on." He glances back at the piece, mumbling under his breath and for a second, I think he said lucky bastard, but I dismiss that thought.

We head back into the house, and I lead August to the dining room. Gran brought out her good china for this occasion, making me smirk. I bet if that woman was my age again, she would tie down one of these guys. The voices get louder as we get closer and when we enter the doorway; Gran is placing a large bowl of salad on the table, next to a larger bowl of pasta and a plate full of perfectly cut garlic bread. Two large men face away from me, but when Gran looks up, she beams.

"Aww. There she is." The two men turn around, one being the Lover boy who loves cookies and the other.

"This is Trin-" Gran's words are interrupted by the second tall bastard.

"Cupcake?" He frowns in my direction, giving me a once over like he can't believe what he is seeing.

"Lucifer!" I screech equally in disbelief. This can't be happening. He was supposed to be a one-night stand stranger, never to be seen again. But no, the universe had to turn around and try to fuck me up the ass with no lube.

Lover boy looks back and fuck, confusion splayed across his face. Did Dante not have a locker room session with his brothers? I take a closer look and notice they all look nothing alike but push that thought back. I have more important shit to deal with. I glare at the devil bastard as his frown turns into a smirk of satisfaction. See asshole.

Chase, as if finally catching on to something, gasps. "No way. Her!" So much for no locker room talk.

I glance back at, hoping she hasn't caught on, but the old bat is grinning ear to ear in amusement. If she thinks she is getting to plan a wedding or something soon, she is sorely mistaken. A funeral, maybe because I believe I will kill this smug bastard.

CHAPTER EIGHT

CHASE

The front door closes as I shove another chocolate chip cookie in my mouth. I almost moan at how good they taste. Probably the best I've ever had. I wonder if I can persuade whoever made them to make me some more. August walks back into the kitchen, looking a bit out of sorts. He looks up at my horde of cookies and scowls. "Those are for all of us. Don't be a dick and eat them all." I gasp at the insult, but I inhale too quickly and the cookie goodness gets sucked back into my throat, choking me momentarily. August, being the good brother that he is, rolls his eyes but steps up and slaps my back, making the killer cookie bits dislodge. I inhale a gulp of air before throwing myself into August's arms. The asshole lets me fall to the ground, making me groan as my tailbone hits hard. "Asshole," I mumble.

He simply shrugs before wrapping up my cookies and placing them in the microwave for later. "So, what was that all about, and can I call dibs?" I bounce on my toes in excitement. The guys and I have traveled a lot and seen some pretty girls. And fucked some even hotter. But that woman at the door a moment ago was something else. Plus, she brought me cookies! She was perfect.

"No, you can't call dibs, plus she already turned you down," August smirks at me and I huff. She doesn't know that her turning me down only made me more interested. I'm like a predator who likes a good hunt. "That was Trinity, our new neighbor. Her Grandmother has invited us to dinner." My ears perk up at that. "I accepted, and you will be on your best behavior," August warns, sending me a stern glare, but I just roll my eyes and hold up my hands.

"Best behavior. Yeah, yeah, yeah. If her food is as good as her cookies, then I'll be the best Boy Scout ever." I raise my three fingers with my right hand and place my left hand over my heart, making August snort.

"Chase, you were never a Boy Scout." I give him a horrified look, clutching my imaginary pearls. "You are exhausting. Go get ready, because I think we're about to have a very interesting night." He stares off toward the front door for a second before smiling. I eye him suspiciously because if he thinks he can call dibs on the hot neighbor chick after I already did, he has another thing coming.

I decide I'll just have to one-up him and be the best gentleman that I've ever been. No one can resist my charms in the end. Trinity is just used to these small-town boys who probably couldn't find her clit with a map. She just needs one night with me, and she will be all mine for the rest of the time we are here.

I took a quick shower, washing in record time, before drying off and standing in front of my closet. I had put everything away a bit earlier, feeling the need to be settled. I look at all my clothes, hoping the perfect outfit will pop out to me. I know I'm good-looking and don't really need to try all that hard, but I saw the way August looked at her. I can only imagine how Dante will react to her; he did just get his dick wet recently, so maybe he is out of the running. Regardless, my brothers are as good-looking as me, so I may need to put a little more effort into it than usual.

As I flip through my dress shirts. I land on a baby blue button-up and grin. Perfect. This color makes my baby blues pop. If I can get her to focus on my eyes, I can get her to focus on other things. Like my mouth and how I might feel between her legs. I didn't get a full look at her, but I saw her honey blonde hair, creamy skin, and curvy body. All on my perfect woman check-list. Add in the fact she denied me, and she almost checks off all my boxes.

I grab the shirt, adding a plain white tank top under and ordinary faded blue jeans for the bottoms. I don't want to seem desperate or anything. I finish my look with my black high tops. Classy but totally ready to throw down. I finish my entire routine with a spritz of cologne and a comb through my unruly hair to give it that 'I don't give a fuck' look that chicks dig. I give myself one more glance in the mirror before blowing myself a kiss and a wink. "Go get her, you bad boy." I purr to my sexy reflection before turning and heading for the door, but end up stopping in my tracks when I see Dante and August's bulky figures in the door frame.

Both men were similarly dressed to me. August in a gray button-up and jeans, and Dante in his usual black attire. I grin, knowing I'll stand out in a more colorful shirt. I notice both guys are holding back a laugh when I cock a brow in question and ask, "What?" At that, Dante and August burst into laughter. I eye them with concern for a few minutes before Dante speaks.

"Did you seriously just tell yourself, 'go get her, you bad boy'?" He chuckles again, but I toss my shoulders back and hold my head higher.

"Yes, I did. I already called dibs, so don't bother encroaching on my territory." I puff my chest, making myself larger. I'm not small by any means. Dante is still a fucking beast compared to me and August. Both men roll their eyes in annoyance, but I think it's a sign of their affection for me. They constantly do it, so it must be them saying they love me in a brotherly way and not in a lover way. Not that I would take them to bed because I swing for team V and not team D and B.

"I already told you she turned you down and you can't call dibs. Dante hasn't even seen her yet. Now, if you're done preening your feathers, we are going to be late for dinner." August states, turning and heading down the hall. Dante just shakes his head and nods. "Let's go Prima Donna." I follow behind, knowing I'm heading to the food finally.

We make our way across the lawn and up the steps to a lovely single-story home. August gives the door a few knocks and while we wait for someone to answer, I give the area a once over. Their front yard has two enormous trees, one on each side of the walkway. The leaves have turned from bright greens to pale yellows and burnt oranges. The sun has set in the horizon, making small streams of fading sunshine light the darkening yard. I turn back to the front door when I hear a scuffle on the other side, right before the clicks of locks being undone are heard. A second later,

71

the door opens, and my eyes drop to an older woman, wiping her hands on a dish towel. She smiles up at us as a small piece of gray hair falls onto her face.

"Oh dear. You all must be the gentleman who moved in next door." She eyes each of us as her eyes grow with excitement. For what, I don't know, but the scent of food fills my nostrils and everything else fades as my stomach chooses that moment to roar out loud. Dante and August glare at me as the little old lady frowns, shooting a look at my stomach. Suddenly, a grin lights her face. "Well, at least I know my food won't go to waste. Come in, come in." She waves us all in, Dante taking the lead as usual, with me taking the rear. "You all must be starving after all that moving and lifting." We all nod before August speaks.

"Yes ma'am. Thank you for the invitation. I hope we aren't causing you any fuss." I cock a brow at the good boy act. He ignores me.

"No fuss at all. I love cooking for people. I just never have anyone to cook for other than my granddaughter. You boys are always welcome here for dinner." She gives us a big smirk as she eyes us up and down. I wink as she gets to me, making her cheeks blush. Dirty little bird.

"Anyway. Dinner has a few more minutes." She goes to turn before pausing and placing a hand on her chest with a shocked look on her face. "Oh my. I'm being so

rude. I'm Betty Black, but everyone just calls me Gran."
She winks and then waits for us to reply. I decided to
take the lead on this one. I step in front of her and grab
her dainty hand in mine.

"I'm Chase." I bring her hand to my lips, kissing the
back of it before nodding to the others. "The big one
is Dante and the other, charming one, is August."

"You're going to be trouble, aren't you?" Is her reply,
but I see the twinkle of amusement.

"Only the best kind."

"Enough Romeo. I'm sorry, Miss Black. Chase thinks
he is irresistible to all women." Dante says, but Miss
Black just laughs, waving him off.

"Please, just Betty and I don't mind. It's nice to feel
appreciated every once in a while. If I was your age, I
would give you a run for your money. Now come along."
She waves us forward, and I grin at my brother, giving
them the "see, I told you I'm a lady killer" look.

We enter a dining room with a table in the center,
with a fancy plate setting all setup. "Take a seat anywhere. Can I get you boys a drink? My granddaughter
has some beer or wine, if you prefer." She pauses, looking behind us in thought. "Speaking of, would one of
you please go grab her? She should be in her art studio
in the garage." August perks up like a damn prairie dog
at the word's art studio.

"I can grab her. Which way?" he asks, looking a bit too excited at the aspect of seeing someone else's art space.

"Down the hall and to the left. Knock before going in. She is probably lost in a new piece, so she might not hear you." She points in the direction he should go, and he takes off like a racehorse. Turning towards us, she gives us a smile that reminds me of a grandmotherly smile I've heard about. Not that I would know since I've never had a family except for these guys. "Now, drinks?" She asks again.

"Beer is fine. If your granddaughter doesn't mind. We can always buy her more if that's the case." Dante replies. Betty waves her frail hand in our direction.

"Nonsense. Don't you boys worry about it? I think you'll like my granddaughter." She smiles, but I swear she mumbles, "Heaven knows she needs more people who like her." But it was so low, I could be wrong. "Anyway, let me go grab those drinks."

We stand there a tad awkwardly, waiting for Betty to return, but a minute later she returns holding a small tray of beers and setting it on the table. "Food's ready, so find a seat, and I'll bring everything out."

"Do you need any help?" Dante offers, but Betty simply waves her hand at the table and heads back towards what, I assume, is the kitchen. She makes three trips, bringing in a large salad bowl, a plate of streaming garlic bread, and last, the biggest bowl of spaghetti I've ever seen.

Dante and I are still standing, since we didn't know if Betty and her granddaughter had certain seats they preferred. I didn't want to assume they didn't and get on the wrong foot with Trinity. I hear footsteps coming from behind me when I turn and see the sexy blonde from earlier.

"Aww. There she is. This is Trin-." Betty starts to introduce us again when I see and feel Dante tense next to me.

"Cupcake?" He says, and I snap my head in his direction and see a small confused frown mar his face. What?

"Lucifer!" Trinity screeches, sounding like a damn banshee, making my head whip back in her direction. Lucifer? Do they know each other? Dante looks surprised, but Trinity looks like she is about to blow steam from her ears as she glares at my brother with disdain.

I look back and forth between the two as August gives a small grin. How do they know each other when we have been here less than a day, and why did she call him Lucifer? Dante's frown turns to a smirk, and it clicks when I see the slight bruise on his face.

I gasp at the realization. "No way. Her!" The pint-sized ball of fury he had heart eyes for and that nearly broke his face is Trinity. I almost don't believe it, but then something else he said confirmed she is the girl. He said she was a fucking goddess with the most intense eyes. That one was a bright crystal blue and the other an earthly emerald green, but I hadn't noticed them earlier, being too focused on the plate of cookies. But I notice them now. Her eyes flare as she glares daggers at Dante, before Betty breaks the tension by clapping her hands.

"Oh, goody. You know each other already. Let's sit and you can tell me all about it." Betty takes a seat at the head of the table as Trinity takes a deep breath before heading to the other side and taking her own. This time when she looks up at Dante, it's with a glint of mischief and excitement flares in my blood. Oh, this should be good. I follow suit, taking a seat across from the troublemaker and wink. Dante pulls out the chair next to me, while August moves to sit next to Trouble.

Once we're all seated, Betty nods and smiles. "So, how did you two meet?" She asks, making me pout for a second. I'm a little jealous of D for meeting her first, but I still call dibs.

Chapter Nine

Trinity

If I could glare actual daggers from my eyes, I would aim them at the ridiculously handsome asshole standing all smug-like in my dining room. The universe has truly and utterly ass fucked me in this situation. It hasn't even been twenty-four hours since the spontaneous fuck session with a stranger; now I find out said stranger is my new neighbor, and he has two equally hot so-called brothers. I know they aren't actual blood brothers because they look nothing alike. It's probably some guy bullshit where it's I have his back, and he has mine bromance.

Gran is wearing a huge grin on her wrinkly face, and the glint in her eyes tells me everything she is thinking. She thinks one of these guys and I will have some grand babies at some point. But that will never happen. When Lucifer's smug lips turn up just a bit at Gran's words that we know each other, an idea pops into my head. My icy glare suddenly turns into a mischievous smirk of my own as I head across the room and take my seat next to Gran. The guys all follow my lead, with Lover boy sitting across from me, Picasso to my side, while Lucifer takes up the seat next to Chase. The smirk that was there a moment ago falls as he takes in my changed demeanor.

Yeah, that's what I thought, Lucifer. Even the devil can fall from his throne.

Once we are all settled in our seats, Gran nods and asks, "So, how did you two meet?" Beaming as she takes in each man with a spark of appreciation. I bet if Gran was their age again, she would be all over them like a monkey to a damn tree. I give the table a once over, eyeing the delicious feast that Gran cooked tonight. At least I'll get good food from all this. "Well, Gran, Lucifer over there." I point in Dante's direction as his jaw muscles tense. I continue to pile a mountain of pasta onto my plate before I continue. "We met at the beach earlier today and I thought he was a random stranger passing through. It seems I was wrong," I mumble the last part as I grab several pieces of garlic bread. "Anyways, I had an itch I needed to scratch, so I thought, what the hell, I'll never have to see this man again." I shrug, grabbing the salad tongs when I realize the room is silent. I look up and find Gran's eyes a bit wide, but a small grin tipping up her lips. Chase's eyes are full of restrained laughter, while August's eyes are assessing. Dante's eyes are a mix of heat and anger, and it is doing all sorts of bad things that should not be happening at the dinner table while next to my grandmother.

I look away from his steel-gray eyes and focus back on my story time. "Anyway, I took him down to the best hookup spot on the beach. What was a few minutes of pleasure with a stranger to live on the edge of life, right?" I shrug. "So, Lucifer went down on me. 10 out of 10 would recommend it if he wasn't such an ass." I say, just as Chase is taking a drink of his beer. He spits out his drink at my words, barely covering his mouth and saving the food, then lets out a hyena like laugh. August chuckles lightly while Dante puffs his chest like he is proud of my 5-star rating and, not hearing that, I still think he is an asshole. Gran hands Chase a napkin to wipe his face, but the woman seems unfazed by any of my words so far.

I smile at Chase as he finally gets his laughter under control, and I continue. "So yeah, he goes down on me, then fucks me senseless for a few minutes. You know, with all the fireworks and whatnot. So, then he gets up, his phone rings, and he has to go. Which is cool because that's how I wanted it. I hadn't even given him my name." I look over at Dante, still looking smug and all proud. "Then he grabs his wallet and offers me money like I was some cheap whore." I smile when his smug grin drops at Gran's gasp. She looks back and forth between us, mouth popping open and closed like a goldfish, wanting to say something but not knowing what.

Dante jumps in before she can. "That's not what it was for, and you know it." He growls, making me cock a brow. I know it's not what he meant, but I'm still pissed. He turns to Gran before softening his face. "I promise I didn't mean to disrespect your granddaughter, but after what we did, I realize we weren't safe about it. I was giving her money to get a morning-after pill, so she didn't have a kid with a man she was having a one-night stand with. To be fair, she punched me in the nose as payment for my words to her." He shifts his eyes to me and gives me a wink, making me grin when his bruised nose shines under the dining room light.

"Too bad I didn't break it," I mumble, shoveling a large bit of pasta into my mouth as the guys plate their own dishes.

Dante snorts. "Maybe next time." My eyes turn to slits, but before I can make a snarky remark back, Gran claps her hands in excitement.

"This is just like in one of the romance stories I've been reading. I think it's an enemy to lovers' books. That's what the young lady said at the library the other day. I'm at the part where the female is injured and the man she hates is coming to her rescue." I stare at my Gran like I have no idea who she is. *Was she body snatched?* I blink at her as she plates her dish, all smiles, until Chase breaks the stunned silence in the room.

"Betty, will you marry me? You're a woman after my heart." I snap my eyes to Lover boy, who holds a smile on his face as he chews a bit of pasta. Gran, the flirt that she is, just winks at him. Before looking up and smiling softly, a glint of laughter in her light blue eyes. "Now that was an interesting story and a hell of a way to meet, but let's all eat before it gets cold. We can get to know each other a little better." I shove another bite of bread into my mouth, staring down at my plate. This was not how telling my grandmother how I met our new neighbor was supposed to go. She was supposed to rage at the treatment of her granddaughter and demand they leave this house at once. Right now, Gran looks delighted with our new company, making me wonder what the sneak old bat is really up to now.

The rest of dinner goes by better, except for Gran trying to get the guys to tell her their life story. The woman could talk anyone's ear off, but I'm glad the three men were gentlemen about it. She made sure they each had two plates, but Chase was basically licking his plate clean when Gran mentioned a chocolate cake she made for dessert. His head snapped up, and I swear his entire demeanor changed to an overly excited golden retriever, told they were about to go for a walk. He practically bounces in his seat as Gran giggles fill the room as she heads to the kitchen.

"I think I'll go help her." I quickly stand and race after Gran, not wanting to spend any more time with the handsome asshole Lucifer, the charming Lover Boy or the intriguing Picasso. All three men are dangerous to my health or maybe sex drive, and I was always taught never to play with fire.

Gran is at the counter making sure her cake looks perfect for her guests as I step up next to her. "Okay, what are you playing at, woman?" I glare at her in question. Annoyed that Gran almost seemed to encourage me to tango with one or all three of the men we just met. I know Gran lived a crazy life before she settled done with my Gramps, but she can't honestly be suggesting I fuck all three men. Confusion replaces my glare as the eccentric old woman fixes me with an intense stare.

"You listen to me, young lady, and you listen good. I see the way all three of those men have been looking at you tonight. I'm old, not blind. Maybe the three of them might be just what you need in life." She points her finger in my face for added effect, and I'm currently too stunned to reply. My mouth is practically on the floor at this point. "You have always had a wild soul and something inside yourself that most people just won't understand. I think these three will understand perfectly. I love you, Trinity, but sweetheart, you need to open yourself up to people and live life."

"But Gra-" She slashes her hand through the air, cutting me off mid-sentence.

"Don't you but Gran me. You forget I know what happened that night. You, my dear, need those men in your life. I know because it's a grandmother's intuition. Now we are going to invite those boys over for dinner every night until you realize I'm right." She spins, picking up the cake, and nodding to the counter. "Grab those small dessert plates and forks." She starts to head back to the dining room, but pauses to look over her shoulder with a smirk. "Plus, in the book I'm reading, they kept getting pushed together until they accepted they were madly in love with each other." Then she heads out the doorway, leaving me completely shocked by this body-snatching woman and her words.

After a long second of frustrated thoughts, I follow behind, dragging my feet, in complete denial that Gran is right. I fucked one of these guys, and it was incredible, but the man himself was a dick. I can only imagine what his "brothers" are like. No. Gran is wrong, me and those guys won't be a thing.

CHAPTER TEN

TRINITY

It's been a week of enduring Gran's not-so-subtle attempts at trying to set me up with one or more of our new neighbors. I think her newest library book check-out is giving Gran some very unconventional ideas. She mentioned that in her current spicy read -her words, not mine-the main female realizes one guy couldn't be enough for her. That each guy in her harem completes a distinct part of her. So now she thinks I need my very own harem. The thought of this is down-right hilarious, but also a pussy clenching thought.

UGH, why do they have to be so damn fucking hot?!

Gran has been this constant nagging in my ear. 'Oh dear, why don't you go ask one of the guys if they can clean the gutters for us? Sweetheart, can you see if one of the boys can change that lightbulb in the hall? Trinity, could you see if the boys could rake up the leaves in the yard?' The woman is relentless. I can picture her watching the guys get sweaty from yard work, offering them a glass of cold lemonade and a pat on the ass for a good job; as her shirt subtly slides off her shoulder. Why couldn't I have an anti-social grandmother who told me boys are bad, that they will only break my heart. Not one to encourage me to pursue three men at a time.

So this week I have cleaned the gutters out, brought the ladder in, to change all the hallway bulbs, and am now currently raking up the yard of all the fallen leaves that come with the season change. All this because I am an independent woman, just like Destiny's Child sang back in the early 2000s. I continue on with the tedious task, making sure to keep track of the time since I work the late shift tonight.

I have my headphones in, jamming out and trying to forget all about them when hands grab my shoulders. Instantly I drop the rake, spin and face my attacker head on. I don't think, I just send a punch to the large chest in front of me, hard enough to make the mountain of a man stumble back. The large body trips over the small sidewalk leading to the front door before letting out a slew of curse words.

Adrenaline pumps through my veins as I prepare for some sort of another attack, but the man on the ground starts laughing. The red haze that was forming begins to fade as my eyes focus back on my surroundings. The asshole who grabbed me continues to laugh as I take one last deep, calming breath.

I'm not being attacked. I'm fine. I'm here.

After reminding myself of my mantra, I glare down at the asshole who just missed a kick to the dick when the figure grins up at me with perfect, bright white teeth. Baby blues stare up at me with pride and desire, making me rethink the kick to the balls. Chase lies on the ground, holding his stomach where I punched him, as his laughter slowly dies down.

"You idiot! What the fuck were you thinking?" Taking another deep breath, I reach down and reluctantly help the big ape up. "You know, I was about to make sure you couldn't have kids anymore. You don't go around grabbing women like that." He flinches at my words and reaches down to cover his family jewels as if I still might. It's tempting, but I'm not that cruel.

"To be fair, I was calling your name, but you weren't answering. At first, I thought you were purposely ignoring me, but then I thought that couldn't be. I'm your favorite." I cock a brow at that, but he shrugs with a smirk plastered on his face and continues on. "Anyways, I moved closer to make it impossible to ignore me when I saw you had headphones in. So I reached out to you to make my presence known, but then you reacted and suckered punched me. Good form, but damn woman, that hurt." He rubs at the spot I must've hit and pouts.

God, the bastard even looks cute, pouting.

"Okay. Well, I'm not sorry for punching you. I might have been if I kicked you in the balls or something, but you deserved it." Smiling my sweetest, fakest smile, I turn, picking up the rake to finish my little project.

"Ouch. Do you kiss your mama with that mouth?" He says, smiling just as big as I was a second ago. At his words, my smile drops and my blood turns cold.

"No. My mother's dead. My father killed her." I turn my back on the asshole, deciding I can finish raking the leaves tomorrow. Memories of that night try to filter in, but I force them back. I cannot fall apart again. Not here. Not now.

"Shit. I didn't know Trinity. I'm sorry." I don't bother with a reply. I need to paint or run now. Yes, run. As I checked the time, I breathed a sigh of relief, knowing that I had some time before I had to be at work. A quick run to the lookout and I'll be back to my regular antisocial, bubbly self. I start for the house to switch my shoes, since I'm already in leggings and a light jacket. The faster I run, the faster the memories fade.

"Wait. Where are you going? I came over to ask you something." I can hear his footsteps crunching the remaining leaves on the ground as he follows behind.

"What Lover boy?" Not giving him any attention, I open the door and grab my running shoes. I kick off my garden boots before calling out to Gran. "Gran, I'm going for a run to the lookout. I'll be back soon." I hear a faint reply of be safe. As I step back out, I notice Chase is still standing there, a curious expression on his face. Damn, I figure he would have left by now. I take a seat on the front steps, then slip into my shoes, making sure they are tied tight. I proceed to do small stretches, preparing for the muscles I'm about to work, when I watch Chase do the same.

"What are you doing?"

"I'm going for a run. I figured I'll take a run with you, and you can show me what this lookout is." He grins that panty dropping smile that all women love, but I just glare at the charming bastard.

"No."

"Yes." He reaches down to touch his toes, and I can't help that my eyes just so happen to notice that he has a nice bubble butt. I also notice that he is already dressed in workout attire, suggesting that he was in the midst of exercising or preparing to start. Or just lazy like me.

"No." I say again because this is me time and the last few nights having dinner with these assholes -on Gran's request - Chase has been a non-stop flirt. Who knew certain words whispered in a seductive purr could make my skin tingle. I've been riding the edge of sexual insanity this last week because of these guys. I even need a new battery-operated boyfriend because I've overused my current one. I can't handle being around these guys for any longer than the mandatory dinner that Gran forces me to be a part of. They are a danger to my hormones and future sex life. I don't even know if I'll get over the way Lucifer used my body. Minus the asshole move afterwards and it was perfect. Rough, dirty, and the O's were just seeing stars.

Fuck, I'm totally ruined now.

"Look Kitten," I arch a brow at that nickname. "You're all small and cute looking until you get close, then your claws come out." He points to my body before miming claws, then shrugs, making me snort. "I know you're pissed at D for the way he acted, but he's always an asshole. You shouldn't assume me and Aug are too, just because we all live together." He pauses as I take that in. I have to admit, he's right—I unfairly grouped them all together as assholes. All because Dante had to be the devil himself. My shoulders slump, and I'm about to half ass an apology when he speaks again. "Also, I want to make something obvious because Betty brought up one of her books last night. The guys and I are not together. In any way!" I frown, not understanding. "Betty was talking about a certain scene she had just read. I think you were in the bathroom or something." He shakes his head in thought. "Not relevant. Anyway, she brought up something called a reverse harem. I had no idea what it was until she explained. It's when a woman has multiple men, but she also brought up how sometimes those men also, you know." He makes a circle with one hand and pokes a finger though in the universal sign for fucking but frowns.

"Wait. That's not right." He continues to place his pointer fingers together. "Nope, that's not it either." He looks back at the front door like he might consider asking Gran what the correct way it would work before I can't contain myself any further. My laughter bursts out of me, shocking him into silence. I haven't laughed this hard in years. Tears fall down my cheeks as I attempt to gulp in air to expand my lungs. It takes me a minute to control my giggles before I can finally speak.

"Got it, Lover boy. You don't cross swords." His face scrunches up in disgust, making another round of giggles escape. "Before you went on that little rant, I was going to say you were right. I refused to get to know you before I gave you a chance. So now is your chance. I'm going for a run to the lookout point up on that hill." I point to said hill, so he knows what I'm talking about. "It's a rough trail, but the view is great. Want to come?"

"Ooohhh, I wanna come, alright." He reaches down and adjusts himself in his gray sweatpants. Motherfucker, how did I not notice those earlier? Gray sweatpants are like every woman's kryptonite. I let my eyes roam up his body to see what else I might have missed. A painted on black band t-shirt and light sweatshirt similar to mine. I can also see his 6 pack as clear as day, making me think of one of those old fashion washboards. Ha, that's where it comes from, washboard abs. "See anything you like?" He purrs, the low seductive tone wrapping around my body, causing my pussy to take notice. God-damn it.

"Keep up. I won't be responsible for you getting lost and eaten by some wild animal." Turning, I head for the back of the house that leads to the trail, heading up the huge hill. I hear him chuckle before footsteps follow behind. This is going to be an interesting run, I can just feel it.

CHAPTER ELEVEN

CHASE

B aseball. Cookies. Cheese feet. Sweaty old men at the gym. Anything to urge my dick to go down before we hit the small trail Trinity was leading us to. I force myself to keep my eyes ahead and at the tree line, but I'm a weak man. I knew it the moment I saw her at our front door with a plate of cookies in her hands. Giving in to the urge of just one little peek, my eyes instantly snap down to Trinity's perfectly perky ass. The term bubble butt comes to mine, making my thoughts turn dirty once again. I know something that can pop that perky bubble. Damn it.

Puppies. Crying kids. Doctor's office... I exhale as my rock-hard cock finally deflates. With perfect timing, too, because Trinity spins around to face me. "Look, I agreed you could come, but don't slow me down. I have to be at work in a few hours, so I don't have time to keep slowing down for you." I grin at her as an idea forms.

"How about we make a bet?" she cocks a delicate brow in my direction before bending down and double-checking her laces.

"What kind of bet?" She sounds interested, so I need to make it something worth her while. Hmmm. I find my mind wandering as I watch her body gracefully bend and twist before straightening, my eyes unable to look away.

"We race to the top. If I win, I get a..." I tap my finger against my lip, making it seem like I'm deep in thought, but I already know what I want. Then I'm going to make sure I win to get it. "A kiss." I give her my best pearly white panty dropping smile. But as usual, my devilish good looks and charms do nothing for this odd creature. I let my eyes trail over her again for the hundredth time since accidentally scaring her. She is wearing basic black leggings that don't look so basic on her curvy figure. A plain white t-shirt and a thin gray sweatshirt zipped up to the bottom curve of her breast, showcasing the perfect handful of a size.

I got more than I bargained for when I tried to get her attention, but fuck me sideways if that was equally hot. The way she didn't hesitate. Just reacted to a possible threat. It concerns me also as to what has happened to her to be so punch first, ask questions later.

We did research on her after that first night. All three of us knew we wanted to get to know her and more. August and I were already at a disadvantage since Dante got a taste of her first. Bastard has been rubbing it in all week, but I had to remind him she probably hates his guts the most for how he treated her, but we all want to pursue her, which meant a background check. You can never know someone's true intentions for you, and women can be the most unpredictable. Like if you accidentally stick your dick in the wrong hole, and they try to throw a shoe at your head. Or that one time I drank too much and passed out during the middle of fucking a chick. She was so mad; she took all my money and left me a note saying I was a shitty lay. I was so hurt by those words, I almost stopped bringing women home. That lasted about a day, so I knew it wasn't me.

I'm pulled out of my awful memories when a clicking of fingers sounds in front of my face. My Kitten eyes me suspiciously before speaking.

"And if I win?" I'm a dick and I know it, but it just escapes. I laugh, making her place her hands on her hips and pop it out to the side. The cutest fucking glare in her multicolored eyes. I get a bit lost in them as the sunlight hits her face in just the right spot. Her single blue eye suddenly looks crystal clear, like the sky on a cloudless day. Her other single green eye is the brightest emerald gem. I'm sure her glare is supposed to be terrifying and to most I'm sure it is, but it just makes me want to wrap her up in my arms and cuddle her until she loves me. Not that I would. That's weird and what weirdos do. And I am not a weirdo.

"Well, since you won't win, why does it matter?" I smirk as I reach up and stretch out my arms. I feel my shirt raise and I watch as Trinity's eyes gaze down at the exposed skin. Goosebumps erupt on my skin as the cool fall air breezes across my bare skin.

"Humor me." She smirks as she looks back up. There's a twinkle in her eyes now, like she knows something I don't. What she doesn't know is I've explored this trail already and know exactly where to go.

I let my eyes roam her body because once again I'm a weak man and can't seem to keep my eyes off her for longer than a few minutes. "Okay. If by some miracle you do win, which you won't, you can have anything you want."

"Promise?" Is her husky reply. Which goes straight to my dick and this time there is no hiding my cock, straining to meet the new kitty cat. Being the non Boy Scout I was growing up, I hold up three fingers like I did for August a few days ago when I promised to be on good behavior.

"Scout's honor." I wink for good measure.

"So as long as I hit the top of the trail of the lookout point, I win whatever I want?" Her eyes drift to my cock, who is weeping at this point. Crying to be loved and cared for. I nod my head, looking like a bobble head, I'm sure, but I'm trying to not think about what it would feel like to slide between her thighs. To feel her body heat surrounding my cock in a tight hug. Her screams and pleads to fuck her faster and harder until my cock is weeping in pure bliss that only my kitten could give it right now. "Deal." Her voice snaps me out of my wanton fantasy before the air whooshes out of me, making me bend in half to catch my breath. A second later, I'm shoved to the ground while Trinity's laughter drifts off as she takes off up the trail.

Oh, you naughty, naughty minx. Kitten's claws came out to play. The woman just punched me in the stomach and shoved me on my ass. Again. She cheated all to win a bet. I think I might be in love with this woman.

It registers a second later that she now has a head start, and I'm just sitting here on my ass thinking of ways I can get this woman to marry me now. I finally jump up and stalk up to the foot of the trail, cupping my mouth, I yell out to the sneaky little brat. "You can run, Kitten, but you won't get very far. I'm coming to get you now!" I can hear a giggle in the distance as I have a new game to play.

Time to catch a naughty Kitty.

CHAPTER TWELVE

TRINITY

I can hear Chase's predatory tone as his voice echoes through the surrounding woods. "You can run, Kitten, but you won't get very far. I'm coming to get you now!" A thrill runs up my body as the pounding of footsteps follows in pursuit. With a playful giggle, I savor the knowledge that he won't be able to catch me, finding joy in the playful chase that awaits. I grew up in these woods. Spent most summers with my grandmother as a child, and the woods were an exciting place to explore. I wasn't like most kids. I've always been what they call antisocial, but my parents made sure I was different. They say someone's past can taint their future, and I know that firsthand.

The wind blows through my hair as I race past fall trees. Their leaves scatter the ground everywhere; allowing me the advantage of hearing Lover boy's presence as he gives chase. I knew I was going to cheat the moment he brought up the bet. For half a second, I thought about a kick to the dick. Something that would stun him for a lot longer, but I might need that dick soon. Once we started heading to the trail, I realized a run wasn't going to clear my mind fully, so why not use the guy who is obviously into me? From what I can tell from that outline in his pants, I'm in for a good time. Now I just have to make sure I win.

I weave my way through the wooded area, ducking under branches and edging around the rougher terrain that I know will slow Chase down just a bit. "Here Kitty, Kitty, Kitty." My heart jumps in my chest, not expecting Chase to sound so close, but I push myself harder as oranges, yellows, and browns blur the sides of my vision. A laugh builds in my chest at the excitement I feel by being hunted. It's not the scary feeling like running for my life; no, this is a thrilling feeling, almost wild like. I know I'm not the prey. I might be running away, but I'm one hundred percent a predator.

I know I'm close when I see the bend in the trail that leads to the small lookout clearing. Chase's footsteps sound louder, closer, quicker coming from behind me, but I don't dare look back. I've seen the horror movie chases. The girl looks back to see the monster, then trips and gets caught. I will not be that idiot. So I stay focused on the finish line, even when I almost imagine feeling his fingertips grazing the back of my neck. As I turn the bend, the small clearing comes into view just a few feet away. I'm huffing and puffing and there is a slight pain behind my rib cage, but I don't care. I will win and he will lose.

My foot barely touches the edge of the clearing when arms wrap around my middle, tackling me to the hard ground. I close my eyes tight, expecting a face full of dirt, but at the last second the body turns, forcing me to land onto a firm, hard chest with a thump and whoosh of air. I'm huffing even more as I feel the caress of lips against my ears. "Caught you, Kitten." Then the fucker nips my lobe before spinning us so that my body is positioned under him. He smirks down at me with his stunning baby blues before I finally catch my breath.

"What? No, I beat you." I demand, trying not to get lost in his eyes swirling with undefined desire. I feel his chest rising and down, combined with his body heat, cause my core to tingling.

"How about we call it a tie? I'll get my kiss, and you can have what you want." He says all this with a purr, grinding his rock-hard steel erection into my stomach, causing my body temperature to reach critical temperature levels.

"All you want is a kiss?" I ask, lifting a brow because this whole bet reminds me of something little kids do at awkward parties, like spin the bottle and truth or dare. Honestly, it's fitting, since I ran like a little schoolgirl, afraid she was about to get cooties from the boy she couldn't admit she liked.

He nods as his eyes zone in on my lips. Being a brat that I am, I slowly slide my tongue across my lips and watch his focus follow the movement. "Fine, but then I get what I-" He doesn't wait for me to finish as his mouth descends on mine. I inhale his scent of pine and mint, kissing him back as he devours my mouth like a man starved. Not liking him in control, I give as good as I get. He nips at my lips, asking for entrance, which I deny with a push to his shoulders. I get him back far enough until I can scoot back and stand on wobbly legs.

He climbs to his feet, frowning at me with confusion, making me want to laugh. "Drop them." That frown and confused look morphs into a surprised confusion. I point to his sweatpants, now covered in dirt, and point to the ground. "I said drop them." This time he looks around as if he heard me wrong. "You got your kiss, now, I want-" I slowly lower to my knees and gaze up at him, showing him what I want and need. "I want you to drop-" As if being electrocuted, he jerks his pants down to his ankles, snapping back up to stand as if waiting like a good boy.

I crook a finger for him to move closer, and he obeys. When he is within grabbing range, I wrap my hands behind his thighs and yank him to me. I don't waste any time as I grab his steel rod and slam my mouth onto it. Allowing his length to slide to the back of my throat, I hear a surprised gasp, then muttered curse words as I slide him back out slowly, my tongue sliding along the bottom of his shaft. "Fuck Kitten. I wasn't expecting that, and I'm no two pump chump, but that mouth is dangerous. If you keep that up, I'm going to cum far too soon." Dumbass. *Don't boys know those words become a challenge for us?* It's like we women pride ourselves on how fast we can make a man cum. I tilt my chin up, and graze my teeth up his cock, causing his eyes to widen. I smile, letting him know I accept his challenge before sending him to the back of my throat until I gag, but I don't let that stop me.

Reaching up, I grip his balls, massaging them a bit as I fuck his cock with my mouth. His groans fill the clearing as I moan around his length. He's thick, and I am licking his cock like my favorite lollipop. I feel his thigh muscles tense under my palm that's keeping me steady, as his balls draw up, followed by a whispered, "no, no, no, no." A low, long "fuckkkkkkkkk Kitten," fills my ears as his hot cum spills down the back of my throat. I don't stop until his twitching slows. Then, with a resounding pop, I release his cock and sit back on my heels, staring up at the 6'1' all-American boy.

He's out of breath for a second before he focuses back on me. "Did you swallow all that?" I shake my head and stick out my curved tongue, showing him said cum pooling on my tongue before closing my mouth and making it over obvious that I swallowed now. His eyes turn molten with heat as he zeroes in on my throat and its movements. I stick out my tongue once more to show it's now empty and grin. "Fuck, that was the hottest fucking thing I have ever seen." His eyes trail down my body before taking a step closer, dick still on display and glistening with my spit. "My tu-" an alarm sounds from my pocket, making me jump.

Shit. My alarm letting me know I need to leave in ten minutes to be at work on time screams at me. I have a twenty-minute run just to get down the hill, then a shower and the ten-minute walk to get to work. I'm fucked. As I look down once more, I'm saddened to learn I won't be able to ride the big guy. "What's going on?" I shrug, holding up the phone.

"Gotta go. This was fun, but I'm late for work." I turn on my heel, heading to the path again before throwing over my shoulder. "See you around, Lover boy."

Feeling a bit better about my shitty day, I picked up the pace and jogged down the path with renewed energy. Hmmm, maybe blowjobs and sex really do relieve stress. I think I might need to test this theory later.

CHAPTER THIRTEEN

DANTE

I pace the living room, annoyed that Chase has yet to return from his run. He should have been back by now. When I attempted to call him, I found out the asshole left his phone on his bed. What kind of asshole does that? Chase, that's who.

"Will you take a breath and calm down? I'm sure he is fine. He probably ran to the beach and went for an icy swim. You know him." I clench and unclench my fist. While I know August is right and that I should relax, I'm the one who looks after us. I'm the one who would take the first bullet if it came to that. Rounding the corner to the kitchen, I take a seat at the breakfast nook and breath like August suggested.

On my third breath, I hear the front door open, making me jump to my feet and head in that direction. There in the doorway stands a dirty and disheveled looking Chase. Taking a second, I look him over from head to toe. I don't see any blood, but he is covered in dirt with an odd look in his eye that I can't seem to place. "Where the fuck have you been and what the fuck happened to you?" I all but roar at him. *Was he jumped? Why is he covered in dirt? But why does he look so happy about it as well?*

"Brothers!" He announces, throwing his arms out wide. "I think I'm in love." He brings his hands to his chest to cover his heart and bats his lashes like he is daydreaming.

"What?" That was not what I was expecting to come from his mouth. Also love? I almost snort at that. Us in love. No one could love monsters like us. I wouldn't even know what love was. As I think about the crazy possibility of love, a pair of eyes flash through my mind. One a crystal blue while the other an emerald green. Nope. That's lust.

August looks up from the computer he was working on. Since we arrived a week ago, we've been looking for links, or any intel, to the fucker we are hunting and possibly next pickup times. Our boss deals with a shit ton of shady shit. Drugs, guns, hits, but one thing he will not touch is skin. He refuses to work with anyone who deals with it as well and if he finds out you start or lied to him; he sends us. We can't stand it, either. The guy we are here for is in a position of power and had a deal with our boss. We get to use the town's small port to load and unload certain shipments, and in return, the man would get a percentage. Unfortunately, the mayor became too greedy and corrupt by agreeing to let his ports be used to traffic women. Women have gone missing all over the state and surrounding states over the last few months. Small towns where it might be common for girls to want to "run away" on their own to become a big-city woman on her own.

"Kitten, man. I'm in love." I snap my eyes back to my brother as jealousy roars through my veins. She's mine.

"What do you mean?" August asks as he places the computer back down on the couch to make his way to us.

"Explain." I growl at the same time. I know she basically hates me, but I had her first. The woman goes toe to toe with me and never flinches. Most women want a man like me for one thing: a good time. A dirty one-night stand to satisfy their wild side.

Chase, being in his own little world, smiles wide as he pushes past me and August and heads towards the kitchen. I watch as he heads to grab a bottle of water and chugs. Water drizzles down his chin before he wipes his face and turns back towards us in the doorway.

"Well, I noticed Trinity was raking leaves in her yard a while ago, so I went to offer my help. I called out to her, but she wouldn't answer. When I got there, I noticed she had headphones in. I grabbed her shoulder to get her attention, and well- ''he appears to blush for a second before grinning wide. Showing all his white teeth. "The woman has one hell of a right hook. She spun around so fast, I didn't even see the punch coming. She knocked me back, making me trip and fall on my ass." I smirk at that and see August smile and nod approvingly as well. That's my girl.

"Anyway, we talked for a minute and I think I said something wrong. She got upset when I mentioned her mom." He frowns at that, as if trying to figure out why.

"You idiot. Did you even read the background check I sent you?" August glares at Chase like a disapproving father. He has a point, though; he would have read that her father committed a murder suicide while Trinity was a young girl. She witnessed it all. She had trouble after that, but mostly normal teenage rebellious shit. The history we could dig up on her showed she took a self-defense class for a few years as well. Proving the punch to my nose was not a lucky shot.

"I'm sorry. I had other shit to look into. You know, like trying to figure out when the next drop is and how these assholes are picking girls." Chase straightens, holding his head high before his shoulders slump slightly. "Look, I just needed a break and went to go talk to Kitten. I didn't mean to upset her."

"I expect you to apologize and make it up to her." I say, crossing my arms over my chest. If she never talks to us again, I might think about giving him a black eye or something. The thought startles me. I've been having possessive thoughts about this woman since I met her. Well, ever since, she stood up and rammed her fist into my face. Then every day since she says or does something that makes me want to flip her around, bend her over my knee and fuck the bratty attitude right out of her. I know she is only acting like this because it gets a rise out of me. I've never met anyone that I battle emotions for. Do I want to strangle or fuck this woman? It's confusing because I've never wanted to fuck a woman more than once. I'm a one and done kind of guy. Does this make me an asshole? Fuck yes. Do I care? Fuck no. The women all get the best sex of their lives and I get to relieve stress. Simple transaction.

"Well, I must not have upset her too bad." I cock a brow at Chase. The bastard is grinning ear to ear and I want to slap it right off his stupid face right now. We wait a long, silent moment for him to continue. "When I noticed her upset, she decided to go for a run, but didn't want her to leave angry at me. I read in a relationship magazine that you should never let your spouse go to bed mad or upset." Spouse? They aren't even dating, and now she is a spouse? "I made her a bet. If I beat her up the hill to the clearing on top, I get a kiss from her. If she beats me, she could have whatever she

115

wanted." Motherfucker. She probably thought she had an advantage, but Chase has been running that trail since the day we got here.

"Anyway, we were about to go when the Kitten struck. She punched me in the stomach and I went down. She took off, giggling the entire way. And damn, did I hate to see her leave but loved watching her go because the ass on that woman is just..." bringing his fingers to his lips. He does the chef's kiss move. I roll my eyes because any man with eyes could see how perfect my Cupcake, was. "So I take off after her and barely catch her as she reaches the clearing. I got my kiss after a bit of back and forth of who won. We came to an agreement that we would both win. We had an epic kiss before she pulled away. Not gonna lie. Best kiss ever." He makes a dreamy sigh, like some teenage girl with a boy band crush.

"What did she want?" August asks, crossing his arms across his chest. I feel like we are Chase's parents scowling at him after coming home late. The asshole's entire face lights up.

"She made me drop my pants, then sucked my soul through my cock until I saw heavenly stars. She even made a show of swallowing my cum, and it was the hottest thing I've ever seen. I went to return the favor, but then her work alarm went off, and she raced off, leaving me dazed and confused with my pants around my ankles."

I don't think I just lunge for the asshole. "She's mine. You're a fucking dead man." Before I can place my hand around the bastard's neck and squeeze, August jumps in front of me.

"Stop!" I glare at Chase, who sticks out his tongue like a fucking child, only making my anger burn hotter. "Let me get this straight." August holds up his hands. "You want Trinity? More than a fuck doll or someone to break. Your reaction tells me you do, so answer truthfully." He eyes me and I nod. He cocks his brow in question.

I step back, letting both men know I'm no longer a threat at the moment. "Yes. I want her. She's not like the others. I can't explain it, but I need her." August nods before turning to Chase.

"And you? Do you want her more than a good time and a hole to stick your dick in?" Chase stands straighter as well.

"Yes man. D is right, she is different. I brought up the idea Betty had about Trinity having more than one of us, and she didn't seem opposed to it. Maybe she can be "it". The one woman for us all." He looks back to August. "I see the way you watch her as well. You want her as much as we do."

August nods. "Yeah. I feel the same."

"What now?" I ask, because we have fucked girls together but never attempted more than that. "How does it work? What if she doesn't want us all? What if she always hates me?"

"Now we go talk her into hanging out with us, so we can bring up the topic of all of us together. I agree, she is perfect for all of us. The hardest part is that we have to convince her of it, too." I grin at that. I can think of a few ways to convince her.

Chase bounces up and down on his toes. "She's at work right now, working the swing shift. What if we go ask her to a movie night, after, or something? That way, we can annoy her until she says yes." August, and I burst out laughing. That might actually work.

CHAPTER FOURTEEN

TRINITY

God, I hated this job. I hate my boss. I hate the customers. I just hate it. But I need the money, so alas, here I am. One thing that I don't hate is that I don't have to wear a full uniform. We have a t-shirt that is a must wear on shift, but I can wear my own comfy jeans and tennis shoes.

I grab the pitcher off the counter and head over to my section to refill a few glasses. Before glancing at the clock on the far wall. Oh, thank god. Finally, I can take my lunch. I let my tables know that if they need anything, to holler and someone will help them. Heading back to the kitchen, I head to my boss's office. The diner is an older establishment. It's cute in that small town, mom and pop way. It's very 50s in decor with checkered floors and old faded red leather booths. Like I said, older.

I stop in front of Chad's office door, pausing to steel my spine. Chad is a creeper. He thinks because he owns the diner that he owns the women as well. Jasmin, one of my co-workers, doesn't mind the attention, but the one time he attempted to hit on me, I shut it down quickly. Now I get lingering glances and inappropriate remarks, but that's better than him touching me. He also hangs out with the mayor and a few other guys in town. They are all creeps, perverts, and sick fucks. I was out taking late night pictures of the town one night and stumbled upon a horrific scene. The mayor and some other sick fuck grabbed some girl off the side of the road. I took pictures, but they were too dark to see the second man's face, but I heard his voice. Missing posters of a teenage girl went up two days later, but after a week they started saying she was a runaway. I couldn't go to the police, since I've seen the chief and mayor having drinks together before. I've taken plenty of other pictures since then as well. Just waiting for the right time to use them against the sick bastards who think they can get away with this.

I let out the breath I was holding before I finally knocked. When no one calls out to hold on or to enter, I sigh. The asshole probably went home early today. He never tells us when he is leaving, so now one of us will have to stay late to close. Which I already know will be me since I was 30 minutes later. Fuck it. I like the after-hours solitude, anyway. I head back to the busier kitchen, letting the cooks know I'm going on break in a few, before I go to find Ali. Ali is my age and a ball of fire, and really the only one I get along with. She is 5'7" with long legs and a curvy body. She has fiery red hair and beautiful green eyes. With her stunning appearance, the woman had the potential to be a top model in a prestigious magazine. However, her shyness and timid nature prevented her from venturing into the fast-paced world of the big city. When I enter the dining area, I spot Ali refilling a customer's coffee.

"Hey Ali. You have a second?" Her head swings in my direction before she smiles and nods. She mumbles something to the guy she was serving, and I watch as his eyes drift down her body and lick his lips. I instantly don't like him.

"Thanks for that. That guy was giving me the creeps. Keeps asking if I'll have a drink with him when I get off tonight." She does a full-body shutter, confirming my suspicions. "Anyway, what's up, babe?"

"Did you know Chad left early today? He didn't let me know, but did he tell you?"

Her shoulders slump. "Yeah, the asshole asked me to stay at night and close." She lets out a deep exhale, and I take a glance back at the creep. He's texting on his phone, but then I watch as he lifts the phone and appears to snap a picture of Ali from behind. Yeah, I have a bad feeling that if Ali stays late, I might not see her again.

"You know what, I'll stay. I was late today anyway. It's only fair." She perks up at that, looking hopeful.

"Really. You don't mind?"

"No, I insist. But I would love to take my break and maybe have a large plate of fries before you leave me in an hour." She beams.

"You got it. I'll go grab you a plate and bring you a cherry coke." As I walk towards the corner booth where I generally sit during breaks, I send her a wink. I can see everything and jump back in if Ali needs me. I doubt she will. She leaves in an hour when we close. Plus, given that it's Sunday night, most people are already safely tucked into their beds, avoiding any unpleasant encounters with creepy assholes.

I just take my seat when the sound of the front door ringing filled the room. Turning to greet who just came in and to ask them to pick any seat, I freeze... Of course, these three had to harass me at work too. I wave my hand around the diner. "Take a seat wherever. The server will be out in just a sec." I turn and plop my ass down on the faded leather bench seat. It creaks under my weight before I pull out my phone to swiftly ignore the guys. Unfortunately, the universe hates me because not even a second later, three enormous men plop down in my booth. I glare, annoyed that my night is even more ruined.

I just wanted to eat my damn fries in peace. Was that so hard to ask for?

"Hey Cupcake." Dante leans in, making me shove my elbow into his gut. A whoosh escapes his lips, a second before Ali steps up to the table, eyes wide in shock. A coke in one hand and an extra large basket of fries in the other.

"Ummm, Trin?" She looks between all three guys before looking over at me with a hint of fear in her eyes.

I let out a long sigh, making all three good-looking bastards smirk. "Ali, these are my new neighbors. Lover boy, Picasso, and this is Lucifer." Chase winks before focusing back on the menu he grabbed. August gives her a small wave before doing the same. Dante, on the other hand, grinds his teeth before nodding in her direction. The moment he shows her a small acknowledgement, his attention immediately returns to me. Now I'm a bit confused. *Did they not see Ali? How are they not tripping over their tongues to talk to her? Maybe they're sick or something.*

"Oh. Ummm, hi." She sets down the drink and basket and slides them to me. "I'll let you three look over the menu, and then come back around to take your order." I nod, letting her know she can go. I wouldn't subject her to the unpleasant company of these jerks.

"What are you guys doing here, and you better not have missed dinner with Gran. I'll never hear the end of it if you did." As I grab the ketchup bottle, I see Dante reaching for my basket. I don't think I act. I slap his hand, making him yank it back and pout as he holds it to his chest. An honest to god pout on this man should be a crime. His bottom lip sticks out, and I get this overwhelming urge to nip at it. But I don't because I'm stronger than that.

"No! Bad Lucifer. Haven't you ever heard of fries before, guys? You never touch a woman's fries unless you wanna die." I give him my best wicked smile before I grab the ketchup and pour some onto my plate. "Look, you have about 5 minutes until I gotta get back to work, so why are you here? I know it's not the food when Gran is next door with a gourmet feast for you "growing boys"." I air quote growing boys because that's Gran's excuse every night she cooked this week when I asked why she needed to cook so much.

The guys all eye each other in the way that screams a secret conversation, but I simply wait them out as I shove fries in my mouth. I hold back the moan that wants to slip free. Gran's food is amazing, but a good old-fashioned greasy basket of fries is just plain orgasmic sometimes. Plus, Gran is on some crazy, health kick lately, and I personally don't want to feel like I'm stealing food from cute baby animals who need green shit to survive. So, I'm going on a veggie strike. I'll even make strike signs if it persuades Gran to consider making more greasy goodness every once in a while.

I must have been lost in my French fries thoughts because when I look up from licking my salt covered fingers, each guy is staring at me with heated desire. Damn it, now my panties are wet because of the yummy fries and these guys. I quickly regain my senses before the guys do, making a show to roll my eyes to the back of my head. "Haven't you seen a woman eat before?"

"No. Most women eat salads and other green shit. Can you eat another fry because that was hot?" August smacked Chase on the back of the head. "Ouch. What the fuck, man! You were thinking it, too." Chase rubs the back of his head, but looks up to wink in my direction.

"Okay, and you're all here for..." I roll my hand to get one of them to fill in the blank. I expect Dante to speak since he always seems to be the head honcho, but am pleasantly surprised when August speaks.

"Look, Trinity, I'm going to be straight with you." I nod to confirm that's what I expected. "I know you haven't known any of us very long, but we want to get to know you better. This sounds crazy, and it probably is, but we all feel drawn to you." I look at all three guys one by one. Each nodding to confirm August words. *What the fuck is going on right now?* "We know you might not feel the same, but I think you feel something towards each of us." I go to speak when he holds up a hand and rushes on. "And I know it's more than dislike or hate that you say you have for Dante."

"So, get to the point. What are you saying?" I continue to pop fries in my mouth, eating them slowly, knowing that each guy is watching my mouth carefully as I do.

"Will you come to a movie night at our place when you get off? We will have food and beer. We can all hang out and get to know each other more." He gives me a soft encouraging smile, but I don't return it. I'm a bit confused, to be honest.

"So, you want to hang out and get to know each other? Why would I do that? I don't like you three."

"I beg to differ." Chase puffs up his chest like a fucking peacock.

"Just because I sucked you off doesn't mean I like you. Women have sexual needs too, and making a guy cum within a minute seems to be a talent of mine." I grin as Chase frowns and mumbles, "it was more than a few minutes," as Dante snorts. So I turn to face him. "Are you saying you didn't cum within minutes of sticking your dick in me?" I cock a brow.

"Do you have to say it so bluntly?" He rolls his eyes. "But fine. Yes, you were squeezing so tight, I doubt a professional porn star could have lasted."

I snort. "I think that was your attempt at a compliment. So, thanks."

"Look. I know I was a dick and I know I don't deserve a chance to make it up to you, but you'll be right next door to your place. You could leave at any time and we wouldn't stop you. I'm just asking for a chance to show you I'm not a complete asshole."

"Oh, brother, you brought a tear to my eye. Kitten, how can you say no to that big softy? Come on, what is there to lose?" Chase wipes an imaginary tear from under his lash before bringing his hands together in a begging motion.

Before I can give the guys my answer, something from the corner of my eye gives me pause. I turn and watch the creeper guy get up before tossing a couple of bills on the table. He winks over at Ali before tossing out a, "See you later, baby." That voice, it sounds so familiar. I watch the guy head out the front door and get into a dark-colored sedan, similar to the one I saw that night. I narrow my eyes on the fucker, a plan forming in my head.

I turn back to the guys and smile. "I'll make you three a deal."

CHAPTER FIFTEEN

TRINITY

D id I really want to have a movie night at my insanely hot neighbor's house? Not exactly, but they said they would have beer, and I think I can manage a two-hour movie. I'll ask them to keep their mouths shut, or I'll leave. Simple. Please, it's free beer and snacks. *What kind of girl would I be if I turned down free shit?*

The deal was simple and straightforward. They would get Ali home safely, and I would spend two hours max at their house before heading back to mine. When I brought up the deal, they seemed hesitant, but I wasn't changing my mind. I have a gut feeling that if Ali stayed late tonight, I would never see her again, and the woman is too good to disappear like that. I can only imagine what those girls who are taken go through, and it's not pretty.

The guys argued with me for a few minutes about one or two of them staying here with me, but I vetoed that real quick. Threatening to cut a dick or two if they hung around. I find it efficient to go straight to the threat sometimes. I could threaten not to come over, but knowing them, they would just invite themselves to Grans and she would allow it. Opening the door with a warm smile and open arms. My own flesh and blood is a traitorous bitch sometimes. They finally agreed with no more added violent threats, which makes me happy.

I hadn't finished my basket of fries because I was in a time crunch to get back to work, so with great reluctance, I push the basket over to Lucifer. "Here, don't say I never did anything nice for you." He looks down at the offering before giving me his devilish smirk, making me roll my eyes. "Now move, so I can get back to work." He stares at me for a second too long, as if trying to see into my soul, before he finally scoots out and lets me stand. My chest brushes against his as I attempt to squeeze by. The bastard doesn't even bother to step out of my way. Before I can get away unscathed, Dante snaps his hand out, gripping the back of my neck, forcing me to look up into his lust - filled steel-gray eyes. He lends down, his breath ghosting across my lips.

"You are the most beautiful creature I have ever set my eyes on." His lips brush against mine in a tender caress before he pulls back. "I'm sorry for how I made you feel that day. Please let me make it up to you, Cupcake." I search his eyes for a moment, almost in a daze, because I can't quite comprehend what just happened. This big bad wolf of a man was just gentle with me. Almost like a whole different man from the one I previously met. His eyes seem to plead with me to give this to him. I'm no weak woman. Men can't just apologize and all is forgiving, but the sincere look in Lucifer's eyes right now makes me feel some unexplainable way. Fuck, I might be weak for these three men after all. I give him the tiniest of nods, and the pleading emotion shifts to excitement. *Interesting.*

I head back to the counter, not bothering to look back at the guys. They agreed to hang out until Ali gets off. Now to explain to her that she has an escort home tonight. Ali walks to work like me, and I didn't see the guys pull up in a car, so I guess they will get a bit of exercise tonight. I quickly make my way towards Ali, who diligently wipes down the vacant tables. We only have two customers left and one of them is the guys, so really just the one couple finishing up. "Hey girl, got a sec?" I call out as she turns towards me with a bright smile on her face.

"Hey." She leans into me, lowering her voice. "Are you with one of those guys?" Her eyes drift to the three men in the corner, making me snort.

"I've fucked one, gave head to one, and the nice one, nothing yet." Her eyes widen at my bluntness, so I shrug. Being secure in my sexuality, I have no issue with casually sleeping with two to three guys. Why do guys get a pat on the back and an atta boy for fucking more than one chick in a week, but the moment a woman does, we are whores? *Total bullshit.*

"No way." She gasps before a smile lights her face. "You lucky bitch. I'm totally jelly right now." She places a hand over her forehead and tilts back dramatically. "Oh, to be young, wild, and free again."

"Ali, we are the same age." I snort, smacking her arm to get her attention to focus on why I called her over. "Anyway, I need to tell you something that you may not like." Frowning, she cocks a brow. "I asked the guys to walk you home tonight." She shakes her head no, but I go on. "Do you trust me?" She pauses at that.

"Yes." Her shoulder slump in defeat, I nod.

"Then trust me now. That creeper guy earlier was bad news. He was showing too much interest in you for my liking. Please, just let them walk you home." I give her my best puppy dog eyes, and when her shoulder slump further, I know I won. "Ali, promise me you won't ever go places alone at night. It's dangerous for us women."

"I promise Trinity." She pulls me into a tight embrace before I push her away.

"Okay, no more sappy shit. Let's finish up as much as we can, so I don't have to stay so late." I turn, heading for the kitchen to make sure they are finishing up as well. While we wait to officially close, Ali finishes up the tables.

Thirty minutes later, I'm locking the front door and flipping the open sign light off. The cooks all left at eleven on the dot, not wanting to stick around later than they have to. Ali grabs her coat from behind the counter. "Are you sure you don't want me to stay, Trin?" I wave her off.

"No. I'll wrap things up fast. I bet I'll even beat these guys home." I wink at her as she pulls her purse across her body, looking nervous and unsure. "I promise I will be fine. Go home, rest. You have the next two days off. Enjoy them." Gripping her shoulders, I lead her to the front door, the guys following behind.

"Cupcake, just let one of us stay with you and walk-" I put my hand up to stop his words. I'm not arguing about this again. I wouldn't be surprised if that creep knew where Ali lived, but his interest in when she got off makes me think he wants to catch her out and about.

"No. She needs more protection tonight than me. Please, just get her home safe." He stops in front of me and frowns. I hate it when he frowns. It doesn't look right on his face. A scowl, yeah, but a frown. Nope.

"What do you mean, she needs more protection than you tonight?" I shake my head. Even if I told them, I doubt they would believe me. Men don't believe women, and I can't trust them like that. I trust them to get Ali home safely. They don't seem like the type to hurt or abuse a woman, but looks can be deceiving. My gut is telling me to trust them on this.

Deciding to avoid the question, I stand on my tip-toes, placing my hands on Dante's firm chest, and my lips against his neck, right below his right ear. "If you're a good boy, you might get a treat." I feel his whole-body shutter at my whispered words. I nip his ear and step back before he can grab me, and we get sidetracked again.

"Promises, promises Cupcake." His heat-filled eyes take me in before he turns towards the door and August steps into my space.

"Please be safe, Little Muse. If we beat you back to our place, we will come and find you. Got it." I nod in understanding as my core throbs at his words. *Holy shit, the promised threat is actually tempting me to be late. Plus, being bad is fun sometimes.* When he turns, Chase steps up next. He doesn't bother with words as he grips my hips, slamming my body into his. His lips crashing onto mine, swallowing my gasp at the sudden but oddly welcomed attack. It's a quick but intense kiss, stealing my breath as he pulls away.

"If you're a good girl, I'll make you purr later, Kitten." He turns towards the others without another word, and I'm just stunned. *What the fuck just happened? And why am I okay with it all?*

I watch them head out into the darkness, all surrounding Ali in a protective circle as they fade into the shadows. I quickly return to sweeping and mopping the floors. While the floors dry, I lower the blinds for the night and finish rolling the last of the clean silverware. With everything wiped clean, put away and ready for the morning shift, I head to the back counter and grab my things. I throw on my sweatshirt, adding my beanie I grabbed on the way out. Heading to the front door, I take one last glance around, nodding to myself, then head out. Turning to lock up, I freeze when the eerie feeling of being watched sends my nerves into overdrive.

I should feel like prey right now; a deer caught in headlights. Frozen in fear, just waiting for my chance to make my escape or worse, waiting for the attack to come, but I don't. I turn the key, lock it up, then toss the key in my backpack. I don't bother with purses. My backpack holds everything I might need: snacks, camera, spare clothes, but most importantly, tampons. Tampons can be used in all bloody situations, menstrual cycles, nose bleeds, stab wounds, just about anything bloody; a tampon can fix it.

I head in the direction of the guy's house, feeling the frosty night air brush against my face. Instinctively, I wrap my arms around my chest, seeking warmth. I'm a woman of my word and will suffer through a two-hour movie since they made sure my friend got home safe. I hum quietly under my breath, making it seem like I'm obvious to my surroundings.

Don't mind me. Just a naïve young woman walking all alone in the dark with no protection. A helpless woman who believes nothing bad happens in this small town. Do-do-do do-do.

It's only a ten-minute walk to my house, so I get to the corner of my street in no time. That's when I hear the crunch of tires on the gravel road side behind me. An engine cuts off before I hear a car door open, then shut. "Hey Sweetheart. You got a second? I think I'm a bit lost." Rolling my eyes to myself, I continue to walk. *I just bet you are.*

The sound of heavy footsteps echoes through the silence, gradually getting nearer, but I remain calm. Men like this strive for fear. If I show any, I'll just be giving this sick fuck what he wants. I can see the guys place a few houses down, but all the lights are off.

Guessing they aren't back yet, I focus on my place. Just a few more steps, and maybe I'll be fine. Being so close to residential houses will surely make him think twice about whatever he might have planned.

I was wrong.

A hand clamps down on my shoulder and spins me around. "Hey. I was talking to you." He sneers down at me. "You know-" He pauses to give my body a leering look. "You weren't the one I was supposed to pick up, but when I told my boss your friend had a boyfriend and friend's walking her home, I told him about you. How pretty you were. I didn't even care if you had that weird eye thing going on. A hole is a hole, after all." His sneer turns into a lust-filled grin, making me want to gag in disgust. It's dark out, but with the moon not hidden behind clouds, I can see more of the man. The sight of him in his all-black ensemble immediately pegs him as the archetype of a nefarious character. *Typical.* His hair looks greasy, as if he added a bucket of hair gel to tame his stringy strands, slicking them back over his head. Dark brown, shit filled eyes gaze down at me as he licks his overly chapped lips. His skin looks dry and in need of at least a gallon of lotion. His whole aura screams perverted, sick fuck, and my gut is usually right.

I take a step back, trying to dislodge his grip, but he tightens his hold. "Where are you going, Sweetheart?

I thought we could do this the easy way. My boss hates when I damage the goods. If I'm lucky, he might let me have a go at you before they ship you off after the carnival." His eyes once more drift down my body. "I have always been an ass guy, and yours looks quite fuckable. I'm sure you could handle a good ass fucking, couldn't you, Sweetheart?" His words send bile up my throat, but I swallow it down. Keep your shit together, Trinity. You can't lose control again. I take a deep breath, thinking through my options. The guys should be here soon, but that might be too late. Fuck.

The asshole reaches around, grabbing a handful of my ass, and I snap. I spit in his face and shove him back. The fucker is a decent size. Not as big as the guys, but bigger and probably stronger than me. "Don't touch me, you sick fuck." The man catches himself at the last second, turning to glare at me. My internal alarm bells scream run, but I can't lead him inside. Gran would be caught in the crossfire of what is about to happen.

I can feel it, the rage building. Just like that night. "You're gonna regret that, you little bitch. I was going to fuck you nicely, but I think you need a rough fuck from a real man to make you heel like an obedient dog. I'm going to make you scream, little girl, but not in pleasure." The look in his eyes tells me everything.

He lunges for me, hands outreached to grab at any part of me, as the rage inside turns my vision red. The asshole moves fast, thinking he could knock me out first as he swings his fist at my face. I don't move as his fist connects, sending me crumpling to the cold, wet ground. My cheek throbs from pain as warm liquid slowly slides down my face. The taste of copper fills my mouth as the fucker sends a kick to my stomach. Air whooshing from my lungs. Get up Trinity. Fight.

I subtly reach for my jean pocket, where I keep my pocket knife. "You thought you could disrespect me and get away with it. I'm about to teach you a thing or two about your bitch." A second later, my hair is yanked back as the jerk starts to drag me. With his back momentarily turned away, I wrap my small hand around my knife, flicking it open from muscle memory, and take one last deep breath before I give in to the red haze.

I'm on autopilot as I reach up to grab the hand gripping my hair. When I have an idea of where he is, my hand holding the knife follows in a slashing motion. I'm abruptly let go, allowing me to spin on my butt and face this guy head on. His curses fill the quiet night air, filling my bloodlust. That's what this red haze is. The craving to harm this bastard, to carve him up and paint using his blood. A brief smile graces my face before I redirect my attention back to the task at hand. I don't wait this time as I jump up and advance, swinging my arm in an arch; my blade landing home in the middle of the asshole's chest. I give him what I'm sure is a twisted, bloody grin as his eyes widen in horror. Maybe it's because he underestimated me, or perhaps it's because he sees the crazy in my eyes right now. I lean in closer to him, the warmth of his blood sliding down my arm.

"Don't worry Sweetheart. This is going to hurt really good." I blow him an air kiss, adding in a wink for good measure as I yank the blade out, watching as he slowly falls to his knees. Blood fills the area I stabbed, bringing me a bit of joy for a second, but then I descend. I lose myself in the red hazy bloodlust, just like that night.

The night I killed my father.

CHAPTER SIXTEEN

AUGUST

"I can't believe you didn't let one of us stay behind to keep an eye on her." Dante whines, kicking at the loose gravel beneath us as we head toward our new rental home. I expected the whining from Chase, not Dante, but I can't say it's not entertaining. He looks like a kid who got told they don't get to have dessert after dinner.

"I'm sorry, but I like my dick and am very fond of my balls. I have a feeling Kitten would know and cut us just to prove a point. We shouldn't underestimate that woman." Chase covers his crotch as he says this and winces at even the thought of testing Trinity's temper.

"I could have kept a distance, stayed in the shadows. Plus, she said something that gave me an odd feeling. I think she might know more about this town and its dealings than we think."

"What did she say?" I ask, trying to think if I've noticed anything out of the ordinary with her. I know she always has her camera on her, so I assume she might have seen something shady at some point, but does she know more?

"She made a comment saying Ali needed the protection more tonight. When I asked her what she meant, she avoided the question. I wanted to push for more, but she forced us out the door before I could." I frown. Ali required more protection? From what? Why? So many questions fill my head. "Then Ali mentioned how her boss had asked her to stay, but Trinity told her she would because she was late." Dante's eyes shift to Chase, who is grinning like a wild man, before he shrugs.

"Now that you mention it, before Trinity asked us to walk Ali home, she seemed tense. The rest of the shift, she kept glancing out the window as if looking for something. Or maybe someone? You don't think she is involved with this shit, do you?" My gut is telling me no, but logically, it would make sense. Sending a woman to meet a new victim is the perfect ploy. Women feel more comfortable with other women. Trinity could lure the girl to somewhere and then bam, you never hear from that girl again.

"Nah man. Kitten couldn't be. Why would she ask us to walk Ali home if she was their next victim?" Chase has a point, but that leads to the question, why did she think her friend needed to be walked home?

"I don't know, but I think we need to figure out what she might know tonight." Dante says, shoving his hands into his pocket.

We walk in silence the rest of the way home but as we got closer to our newest living arrangements; I noticed a car parked on a small side street. I've never seen it on this street before, but we haven't been here that long. This could have been someone out of town or just coming to town to visit someone. I note the vehicle in case it's needed. It's a bigger sedan, dark in color. The windows seem to be tinted dark as well. An uneasy feeling consumes me as we pass the sedan, but I can't explain why. It's just too out of place for my liking.

"I call dibs on sitting next to Kitten tonight. Oh, and on the last of the cookies Gran made earlier." Chase puts a little pep in his step as we get closer to the house.

"Do you think our girl is waiting for us, or do you think we will have to go for a little hunt?" Dante asks with a smirk. He loves a good cat-and-mouse game. We all do. Sometimes we allow our victims to "get lucky" and escape, just to scare them, knowing we could catch them at any second if they aren't fast enough. So far, the cat wins every time.

"Kitten is a wild card. She might test us just for fun." Chase grins at the thought. He's right. I can see Trinity purposely making us come get her just to prove a point.

As we get a few houses away, I pause at a really familiar sound. Flesh hitting flesh rings in my ears, filling the night air with the scent of copper. Blood. Dante and Chase pause as well, hearing the same noise. Then I hear it, a whispered purr. "I told you it would hurt real good." I'm moving within seconds, my brothers' steps behind as I follow the continued pounding of flesh sounds. The sound leads me to the house right before ours. *Fuck.*

I turn at the gate, but freeze as the scene unfolds before me. My eyes take in Trinity straddling a man on the ground, both absolutely covered from head to toe in blood. I whispered, "Holy shit" and "What the fuck?" come from either side of me, but I can't manage a single word. Trinity doesn't seem to notice us as she continues to pound on the unrecognizable guy. I notice a flash of silver as she forcefully slams her fist down yet again.

The image in front of me leaves me speechless, unable to express the mix of shock and disbelief. Trinity looks beautiful, covered in blood, an almost feral smile lighting her face. My hand twitches with the overwhelming urge to paint this scene and hang it on my wall. What if I were to use this man's blood as a medium? Would my Muse think that was wrong?

"Should we stop her?" Chase mumbles. "Also, is anyone else getting Chucky vibes here? I don't call dibs on getting her attention. I've seen the movies. Once you get their attention, they come after you. I like my body parts left inside me, thanks." He whisper shouts, but Trinity doesn't budge as she tears into this guy. I wonder what this guy did to attract such a tragic outcome. Not that I really care, but I'm a curious man by nature. I'm guessing it wasn't good.

"Cupcake?" No reply. "Trinity?" Stab. "Baby, answer me." Stab. "Fuck, why isn't she answering me? It's like she doesn't see or even hear us." Dante grips his hair in his hands, getting more frustrated by the second.

"It's like she is in a daze or something. We need to get her out of here and clean this mess up before anyone sees." Chase says, peering around the area. He's right, but I've heard it could be dangerous to wake someone when they are in a daze-like state. They become confused and unpredictable.

"I have an idea. I need one of you to grab her from behind. She will probably strike out and fight, but hold her tight. I don't want to get stabbed or gutted." Dante nods, a determined look crossing his face as he goes to move into position. I take a deep breath before preparing myself as well, knowing there might be a possible stab my way once Dante grabs for her.

"Ready?" Dante asks in position. I nod, readying myself. I watch as Dante rushes forward as Trinity's arm swings up, preparing for another stab, and he places his arms under her. He quickly pulls her up and away as she lets out a grunt at the sudden movement. I rush forward as her arm swings down to slash at whoever is her next threat, but before Dante can get his hands locked behind her head and immobilized; her blade connects with my shoulder, making me clench my teeth at the sudden flare of pain. The knife gets stuck as Dante's fingers lock into place. Trinity starts to kick and fight to get free as I step into her space. I don't bother with the blade as I reach up and grip Trinity's face gently. I don't know if any of this blood is hers or if it belongs to the now dead guy at our feet. From the corner of my eye, I see Chase leaning over said guy, patting down his pockets, looking for identification and any other information we can find.

I turn back to focus on the woman in front of me. Trinity's breathing is erratic as her chest rises and falls under her blood-soaked clothes. Her once clear, beautiful, mix matched colored eyes now look completely lost as I try to get her to focus back on me. "Trinity. Trinity baby. I need you to slow your breathing. Please, baby? Listen to my voice. Come back to us." The more I talk, the more her breathing slows. "That's it, Trinity. Come back to us. Good girl. Just breathe. That's it. You're safe now." I look up at Dante, who is still holding tight, and nod. He slowly loosens his hold as her body relaxes with every slow, calm breath she takes. When he releases her completely, she stumbles forward, right into my chest, smearing blood all over me as soft sobs begin. I can feel the sudden exhaustion take over as her legs give way, and she practically collapses to the floor. Catching her last minute, I scoop her up into my arms as Dante reaches forward, gripping the knife in my shoulder, and yanks. "Motherfucker. A warning would have been nice, asshole."

"Get her home and start cleaning her up. We will clean this up and be there soon." I don't respond as I turn on my heel and head straight for our place.

"Ugh." Trinity holds up her hands in front of her face as if inspecting the blood like an art piece. Not that I'm complaining, because I, personally, think red looks good on the woman. "No. Not again. Fuck. Not aga-" Before I can ask what she means by not again, she passes out from the adrenaline rush she just had. I make a mental note to bring that up when she is clean and rested.

I balance Trinity in one arm as I open our front door, flipping on lights as I go. Under the fluorescent lighting, I think I see possible bruising on her right cheek, but there is still so much blood. She is practically dripping with the cooling liquid as I head straight for Dante's room. His bathroom has an enormous bathtub I can place Trin in. I doubt she could hold herself up currently, so a nice warm bath it is. Looking down at the tiny woman in my arms again, I lean in to kiss her forehead. "Don't worry, Little Muse. We got you now."

WELCOME
TO

THE
CARNIVAL!

CHAPTER SEVENTEEN

DANTE

I watch as August carries my Cupcake away. The urge to follow them, to protect my woman, rides me hard as August finally disappears behind the front door. *What happened to her?* I knew the woman was perfect, but this just confirmed it. She was beautiful as she straddled the man, bringing down the blade in repeated clean, sharp arches. I know August says Trinity was in a daze, but I saw the smile lifting her lips. She enjoyed the kill.

"Dude, I know you want to go after our girl and check on her, but in order to protect her right now, we need to clean all this up. Now, what are we thinking?" I glance over at Chase standing over the dead man, tapping his chin in thought. "He looks pretty shredded. We could toss him in the woods and claim an animal attack. Or go mafia style and feed him to the fish." He waggled his eyebrows, looking a bit too excited at that thought.

"What did you find on the guy?" Chase hands over a wallet and some car keys. Looking back over my shoulder, I remember passing a blacked-out sedan parked down a way. "Anything else?" I open the wallet to find the bastard's ID. Jimmy Smith. A boring name for a thug. Crouching down, I look over the bloody corpse. He is wearing dark clothing that is now saturated in blood, and it appears my girl did a number on him because his face is unrecognizable at this point. *My woman did good.*

"Take these keys and go check that car that we passed on the way here. Look for a phone and anything else useful. I have a feeling he might have worked for the mayor and his new partner." Catching the keys, Chase heads to grab the car without a glance back. I hear a door creak open behind me, and I freeze. Fuck.

"She doesn't want to admit it, but that girl needs you three." I spin around, trying to make my body cover the body on the ground as Gran stands at her front door. With her hair set in curlers, she is comfortably dressed in a soft bathrobe and slippers. Her eyes glance down at the massacre just behind me before she lets out a heavy sigh. "I'll go grab the bleach." She turns, heading back into the house, and I watch dumbfounded for a minute. *Did I hear her wrong?*

I'm still standing there as I hear a car pull up behind me, then Chase's hurried footsteps rushing forward.

"What the fuck, man! Help me move the body before anyone sees it and calls the police. No body, no evidence." His eyes darted behind me before widening to the size of saucers. "Shit, did Gran see? Wait, is she calling the cops? Fuck. What do we do, D?" Right as he finishes that sentence, Gran calls out.

"Alright boys. You take the body to the car. Then come on back and help me with this bleach." Chase, reacting much like I did, stares at her like a deer caught in the headlights. "Don't just stand there. We don't have much time. Now move." She claps her hands, breaking our stunned stares.

"I'm afraid to ask, but why do you seem so...." Chase looks over at me and I shrug. I don't know how to explain what is going on right now. "...so...so... I don't know. So calm about this?" He points down at Jimmy's body.

"This is not my first rodeo, gentlemen, but Trinity's story is not mine to tell. I'll tell you now, this isn't the first time I've stumbled upon that girl beaten and bloodied. She didn't have an easy life growing up, but she deserves someone to look out for her. I see how you three look at her. You take care of my girl. Do you understand me?" She gives us one of those stern grandmotherly looks and we both nod in understanding. "Now get to work, so we can get this cleaned up, and you back over to that girl."

With that, Chase heads for the top of the body while I reach for the feet. Hauling the body up, we head to the car. The trunk is already open, so we just toss him in, bending his legs to get him to fit, before slamming the trunk shut and heading back to Betty.

"Now one of you grab the hose on the side of the house. I brought the scrub mop, so it won't stain. The bleach just needs another minute or two to set." She hands me the mop as Chase goes to grab the hose. I take a moment to go over everything that has happened in the last 30 minutes. Trinity killed a man. As of now, for unknown reasons, but I'm betting he tried to take her, and she wasn't having it. Trinity also went into a type of daze that had her swinging at anything that came near, including August. Then Betty comes out of left field with a mop and a bucket of bleach, more worried about a stain on her walkway than the fact her granddaughter just killed a man. Holy shit, it's like I'm in some alternate universe, but I'm not even mad about it.

The woman my brothers and I are lusting after is a god-damned bloody queen in her own right, giving me a bit of relief because she might not be so horrified when we tell her what we really do for a living and why we are here.

Betty lets out a long yawn. "Alright boys. I'm headed off to bed. Be sure to clean up properly before you head off to bed yourself. I recommend the cliffs." She winks at Chase and he winks back. She must have overheard him talking about his swimming with the fish's idea. "You four come over for a late lunch tomorrow, and we can all chat." She turns, heading back inside, once again stunning me into silence. Before she fully closes the door, she calls out, "Night, boys." The sound of locks following.

"Well shit. Wasn't expecting that to happen. I'll say it again, I would marry that woman if I wasn't already in love with my Kitten. Now can we hurry? August is getting all the knight in shining armor credit because you know, I helped too? I should get more credit since I'm cleaning and hiding evidence." Turning on the hose, he sprays down the sidewalk while I scrub the more caked on stubborn spots. We make quick work before the idiot has to open his big mouth. "Fuck man. I'm hungry. You know, a good killing almost makes me have cravings." I snort. His craving isn't for food. "I wonder if Kitten is like me and needs a good fucking after a kill?" Then he looks me straight in the eyes and raises three fingers. "I volunteer as a tribute."

"Shut up. Now let's go get rid of this piece of shit and get back to our girl." We take the supplies and toss it in the back seat, while Chase hops into the driver's seat and I grab our vehicle before heading to the cliff Betty mentioned.

Hold on, Cupcake. We're coming for you.

CHAPTER EIGHTEEN

TRINITY

S obbing echoes around in my head as I lift it to see where it is coming from, but I can't manage more than my eyes. My body feels heavy and exhausted, like I just ran 10 miles with no breaks. My clothes stick to my skin, feeling wet but oddly warm. That's when I realize I'm being carried and the warmth is coming from the person holding me to their chest.

"Ugh." I groan, making my head pound even more as I finally lift my head to take in my surroundings. The last thing I remember is the guy from the diner walking up to me, grabbing me, then making disgusting threats. I try to focus on what happened after, but the memories seem foggy right now. Maybe I hit my head. I frown at that because if I passed out, then who is carrying me? August. I remember his face. He was staring down at me with concern, fear, worry possibly, but why? I focus harder, trying to force the memories, but hiss when a small throb comes from my right cheek. What the? I lift my hands to check for potential damage when my eyes catch on the color coating my usually creamy skin. Red. Blood. Lost of memories. "No. Not again. Fuck. Not aga-" Oh god.

I must have overstimulated my brain for a few minutes because when I crack open my eyes next, I'm being lowered into what I'm guessing is a table. August's scent of paint and coffee fills my nose, but it's overwhelmed by the bitter scent of copper. When I'm fully set down, I feel August lean into me before kissing the top of my head. "Don't worry, Little Muse. We got you now." He goes to move away, but I reach out to grab him. I don't want to be plagued by the haunting echoes of nightmares again.

"Don't leave." I peer up at him, hoping he can read the plea in my eyes. He stares at me with concern now, but is it for his safety or mine? I'm pretty sure I just killed that man, but as my eyes lower to August's chest, they widen in shock. His chest is completely saturated with blood, including his arm. He must notice my shock because he follows my line of sight before sighing.

"It's not mine, if that's what you're wondering." He shrugs, then winces, looking towards his shoulder. "Well, most of it isn't mine." My brow furrows in worry now. *How did he get hurt? Or did I get hurt? I don't feel hurt.* A little sore, but nothing feeling like it's bleeding.

In the next second, he tears his shirt off over his head, leaving a bit of small blood spots that soaked through his shirt to his fully tattooed skin. But I don't see any injuries until I spot his shoulder. Blood slowly leaks from a minor wound as I scramble to climb to my feet. Just as I'm halfway up, my left foot unexpectedly slips out from under me. I let out a small shock scream as my arms windmill, attempting to find something to catch my fall. Arms wrap around my waist and yank me up and against a hard chest.

"Whoa there. Slow down, Little Muse. Let's get you cleaned up, okay?" August stares down into my eyes like he is searching my soul. But one thing crosses my mind now that the adrenaline has faded. August is looking at me with more than just worry. It's almost like desire, but that can't be right. He just saw me kill a man. There's no doubt that I'm covered in blood from head to toe, but August doesn't seem to care. "I'm going to start the shower. So you can wash up. I'll be right outside if you need me. Just call out. I'll find you something to wear as well." He looks down at my body, letting me know that I'm right about being covered in blood. August reaches around me, flipping the shower on. Cold water rushes out, spraying my entire side as I rush to shift away from the freezing water. "Shit! I'm sorry. I promise it warms up fast. I'm going to go grab towels." He goes to step away, but I grab his hand, shaking my head no. I don't want to be alone. He doesn't bother arguing, simply nods.

I stand there in the tub, water beating down on me, already turning pink, and I'm not even standing fully under the spray yet. I'm trying to find words to explain what happened. Surely, they didn't call the police since he put me in the tub, evidence running down the drain as we wait. But then why is he helping me?

"Do you need help?" He points to my clothes, but I shake my head. I reach for my shirt, peeling it up as I cringe at the feeling of blood that had already dried. As I get to my shoulders, my shirt gets stuck over my head, since peeling off half wet clothes covered in blood is already awkward enough. Of course, they had to get stuck.

I finally find my voice as I wiggle and do some weird shimmy to turn and get unstuck on my own. "Maybe a little help." I hear a small chuckle before large, warm hands grip my rib cage, making me gasp. August traces his fingers up the sides of my body until he reaches the shirt and slowly tugs it up and off. "Thank you." He drops the soiled clothes on the ground with a plop, his eyes never leaving mine. I go to reach for the button of my jeans, but he beats me to it. Slowly, he unbuttons my pants before sliding them down my thighs. When they get to my feet, I lean forward to grip his shoulders for support, careful not to touch his wound. I step out of my jeans, one foot at a time, until I'm standing before him in a skimpy and now ruined bra and undies.

"Can I shower with you? You know, to save the fishes and shit?" I snort at that, making him smile in return. A dimple appears on his face as he winks down at me. "I love it when you smile." His hand reaches forward to push a clump of hair behind my ear. Fuck, I sense that this is a romantic moment, but I probably look like Carrie or something out of a horror movie, though August doesn't seem to care as he steps closer. "It makes your eyes light up that much more." I'm lost for a second as I stare into his handsome face before a snap of a button and rustle of jeans breaks the hold he just had on me. "I should ask before we get started-" I cock a brow at him. Feeling more like myself the longer I'm around him. "I know you've killed before." I tense. "Don't worry, you're safe, but I need to know, are you the type to sleep it off or fuck it out of your system? The remaining adrenaline, I mean." He bites his lips, waiting for my answer, and God damn it if that is not fucking hot.

Am I fucked up for wanting to tell him the truth? That when I go into what I call the red haze, I either need to fight or fuck to feel better. Fuck it. "I would prefer to fuck it out of my system. Know anyone that could help?" That's when he drops his pants and I get a good, long look at his fully tattooed body. I mean a fully tattooed body. His dick is tattooed, and I really want to trace every dark line with my tongue at some point, but right now, I need more.

"Let me take care of you. Okay?" He steps out of his jeans before he turns me so my back is facing him. "Let us take care of you tonight." A second later, my bra is removed as I'm turned again. He kneels in front of me as he lowers my panties, grazing his fingers across my skin as he goes. Now fully undressed, I step under the water, the droplets cascading down my body, while his hands remain ever present. The warm water pelts my body and the water runs red, but I keep my focus on August as his hands move to my scalp with a handful of soap. I didn't even notice where he got it from, but the moment his hands start to massage my scalp, I don't think about anything else.

I almost moan out at his magic hands as he continues to lather up my hair. Forget, fucking it out of my system now. I just need August's hands doing whatever he is doing now. A few minutes later, he makes me lean back into the spray to rinse, and I give him a pout as he removes his hands. "Don't worry, Little Muse, I'm just getting you clean before I take care of you." He leans down to nip my nose.

Over the next few minutes, August washes my body with gentle hands until the water finally runs clear. He's on his knees as he finishes washing off my feet before he looks up at me with pure lust filled eyes. Slowly, he traces up my legs until he reaches my core. "I've heard you taste as good as you smell. Mind if I have a taste for myself?" He doesn't wait for an answer as he glides his finger through my folds, quickly bringing his fingers to his lips. He groans as I watch him wrap his lips around his fingers, licking my juices off with a hungry look. "D was right. You taste as sweet as can be." He gets to his feet before gripping my hips. "Do you trust me?" That's a good question. I barely know the man, but he did just wash evidence of a murder down his drain, so I suppose a little trust should be given.

"Yes." I meant for my voice to sound confident, but it comes out huskier and more breathless. I'm so turned on right now. From the combination of watching water drip off his inked body, the way his hands explored me with innocence, to the not so innocent way he tasted me. Add in the red haze of adrenaline and the fact that this man and his brothers have been giving me wet dreams all week. Yeah, I'm about to combust if August doesn't touch me soon. Going down on Chase this afternoon after our little cat-and-mouse game just added fuel to the fire of my needy pussy. I don't even think BOB could satisfy me at the moment.

"Good. I need more." His grip on my hips tightens as he lifts my body up, so my pussy is level with his face, before he shoves me to the wall. My thighs tighten automatically around his head as I lock my legs in a loose hold as well. I hear him grunt; I'm guessing from the pain in his shoulder. My mind tells me I should probably ask how he got his injury, but that's not too important at the moment. He descends a second later like a fat kid eating cake as he slams his tongue into my greedy pussy. I often hate the fact that I'm size challenged, but right now, it is useful since when I throw my head back, I don't hit the ceiling. *Maybe being small has advantages.* August goes to town quickly, working me up into a toe-curling orgasm. My thighs doing their best to suffocate this man. He doesn't seem to mind as he continues to lap at my center before he pulls back and grins like a madman.

Without saying a word, he does some quick maneuvering, pulling my thighs away from his face, down and around his shoulders. Then slides me down the wall until my core lines up with his shaft. He doesn't make any move to enter me as he stares into my eyes. We stay like that for what feels like forever, but which is really only a minute or two, before he leans in ever so slowly. He places a sweet kiss on my lips, only pulling back a centimeter. "You will belong to us after this. We wanted to take this slow for your benefit, but after tonight, you cemented our bonds. You're not alone, Trinity. Not anymore. We will explain everything in the morning, so you have until then to accept that. If you try to run from us, we will hunt you, and you want to like it when we catch you. Do you understand?"

His words should send me running and screaming in fear, but my brain and body are both on the same page right now. We want this. We want them. Unfortunately, my brain still thinks we are a sassy little brat and shouldn't bow to any man, so instead of simply agreeing like the good girl I'm sure he wants me to be, I turn up my attitude. *Also known as my sass switch or bitch button.*

I ghost my lips over his. "You know your words do very naughty things to me, but I thought you would be a sweet, gentle lover in the bedroom. You know the flower petals, lit candles, romantic music, the whole shebang. Isn't the alpha hole DOM asshole thing supposed to be Dante's thing?" Batting my lashes up at him, he smirks down at me. It's not a kind smirk, either.

"You want me to be sweet and gentle?" He cocks his head. I blink up at him innocently. "No. You don't want me to be sweet or gentle. I think you want me to slam my cock so far into you that you see stars. You want me to fuck you so hard that you lose your voice from all the screaming and pleading you will be doing. I think you want to be fucked by me and my brothers at the same time." My pussy tightens at the thought, sending my juices down my leg. "I think you wish to be so full you can't think straight. Is that what you want, Trinity? Do you want me and my brothers?" I'm not proud of myself, but I nodded so hard I almost gave myself whiplash, making him chuckle. And oh boy, I didn't think a chuckle could be so damn sexy. "Well then, let me get you all warmed up. The others will join us soon, so let's make you come at least twice more before I have to share."

Before I can get another word out, August is slamming home.

CHAPTER NINETEEN

CHASE

W e walk through the front door expecting my Kitten to be curled up on the couch fast asleep or maybe sitting in the kitchen casually chatting with Aug, but I don't see either scenes. Panic rushes over me as thoughts of a backup guy or someone coming here while we were disposing of the body. It didn't take us long, since this wasn't our first clean-up job, but you never know. I look over to D, who is frowning as he takes in the Trinity-less room. Same man, same.

Nothing looks out of place or like someone who isn't us entered, but once again, you just never know. I tilt my head down the hall. "Maybe they are in one of the rooms. He might have put her to bed or something." I shrug. Honestly, the bastard probably put her in his bed knowing we wouldn't want to wake her up, so he would get Kitten cuddles instead of me. Smart bastard.

I take a step toward the hall to go search for my woman when I hear a bang bang bang sound. My steps pick up as I head further down the hall, D right on my heel. The sound gets louder as we reach Dante's room. Before I can second guess my actions, I fling open the door and step inside. When I still don't see them, I focus on the sound. Bang bang bang. That's when the sound of the shower running and the steam from the crack of the door not being closed pulls all my attention. Bang bang bang. I open the door and freeze.

There in the steam of the room, August's naked form can be seen, but the other person is where my eyes are drawn to. Trinity is being pounded into with force up against the shower wall. Both of them are dripping wet as the water continues to pelt their naked skin. Trinity's moans fill the small space, echoing around in my head as my jaw all but drops to the floor. My cock turning to stone in my pants as I watch my brother fuck my woman senseless. Like I've told Trinity earlier today, my brothers and I have never been with each other, but the sight in front of me might persuade me a bit more.

Both of them are completely lost in their moment as Dante and I stand in the doorway, getting a free erotic show. I almost want to say it was better than porn. I mean, it's basically porn, but in real life. As I glance over at D, I realize he has never been the kind of person to share. He was the kid in the sandbox that would kick the sand in your face, then take what he wanted. *Good times.* Currently, all I see is pure desire and lust as he reaches down to rearrange himself.

I do the same, since my cock is currently trying to pull me to the woman across the room. Begging me to join in, to make her scream my name just as loud as the other. I must make a noise because August and Trinity snap their heads towards us, but without missing a beat, August slams into her harder. "I told you they would be here soon, but I still need you to cum once more before you can have all three of us." He grins at what must be my shocked look. "Little Muse, look what you do to them." Her eyes dart down to my cloth covered cock as her eyes somehow get even more heavy with desire. "Do you want them, Trinity? Want all three of us in you? Filling all of you so full, you will have no choice but to cum with pleasure. Even then, we won't let up. I told you, Trinity. You are ours now. Is that what you want?"

Before anyone can speak, my hand shoots up. "I want that. I want that very much." Trinity's eyes sparkle with excitement as she looks over to Dante, this time in question. The ape simply nods, but that must be enough for her because August reaches down to pinch her clit. She lets out a scream of pleasure, her eyes rolling back, body stuttering as August holds her up. He slows his thrusts as he nods at us. I take the hint first, rushing forward as he slowly pulls out, making

Trinity whimper at the loss of fulfillment. He passes her to me as I scoop her up into a cradling position. "I got you Kitten. Don't worry, we are just moving to a better area. I'll make you purr in no time." She smiles up at me with that sexy, satisfied look. "Oh no, you don't. We aren't done, baby. Not by a long shot." I lay her down on Dante's bed. The man moves to his bedside table and pulls out lube and a few condoms. I look up at him with a cocked brow, in question. August just fucked her bare back, and D did the first time, but now he wants condoms.

"It's her choice. I got punched the last time we fucked, so I'm covering my bases." He shrugs but looks down at the smiling vixen.

"Picasso already said I had tonight to accept this. So, you better get over here and give me a good reason why I should." She spreads her legs, giving us the perfect view of her pretty pink pussy. I waste no time ripping off my clothes and diving between her legs, giving her a single long lick.

"I call dibs." I call out before I dive back in. If I have one night to prove to this woman, why she needs to accept us, then the best way to a woman's heart is to fuck her so good that she will never be unsatisfied. I'm pretty sure I read that in a magazine before. Between the three of us, if this woman can walk in the morning, we don't deserve to have our man cards.

Wasting no more time, I get to work, claiming my Kitten.

Chapter Twenty

Trinity

I thought Dante and August had magic devil tongues, but Chase is making me see stars with just his mouth. It could be because August made me cum twice before passing me along, but what do I know? I feel the bed dip beside me before Dante leans over me.

"Do I get a second chance? I promise not to throw money at you this time." I snort, making him smirk. That damn smirk. Brat mode officially activated.

"I don't know. Your brothers seem to keep me satisfied on their own. What do I need you for?" I ask breathlessly as Chase doubles his effort, working me into a frenzy.

"Oh, Cupcake, you have three holes for a reason. And I think that mouth of yours needs to be filled right now. What do you say? Want to be a good girl and take all three of us, or do you need a few spankings to learn to behave?"

"Oh D, whatever you just said to her, she likes it. A lot." Stupid traitorous body. Freaking praise kink. Fucking spanking kink. Stupid fucking sexy men and their hot as fuck words.

"Oh really? Was it the taking all three of us at once like a good girl? Having you so full that you would be at our mercy. Have you ever taken more than one man at a time?" I moan out as Chase nips at my clit, a zap of pain adding to my pleasure before fingers slowly slide up my folds.

"D, man, she is soaking my face right now. Do you like that, Kitten? The idea of three men at once." I squeeze around the finger he slowly inserts. "You do. How about this?" He drags his finger against my walls until he trails down to my ass. Gently, he presses in, causing me to tense until I feel him cross my tight opening. He leaves me gasping at the intrusion as he gives my core one of his long, magic filled licks.

"Please. Please. Plea-" I mutter, not sure what for, but I need something. I need more. I need these men to stop speaking and just do what they keep telling me. A man of action.

"Please what, Cupcake? Tell us what you need. Tell us how you want us. We are yours just as much as you are ours. You will be our queen after tonight. Do you understand what that means?" Dante leans forward so that all I can see is his face as Chase removes his finger from my ass and mouth from my center. I whimper at the loss of pleasure. I go to complain at him not to stop, but Dante catches my chin, making me keep my eyes focused on him. "Do you understand, Trinity?" His grip tightens, but I shake my head. I don't understand what he is saying, not in my lust induced sex-crazed mind set. He gives me a soft smile and the way he is staring down at me should tell me a million things, but I'm not in the right mind. My brain has shut off, so my pussy is doing all the thinking for us. "That's okay, Cupcake. We're going to show you what it means." I just nod as Dante's lips crash down on mine. The sweet man giving me the creeps a minute ago is gone, replaced by the man I first met. He kisses me with a mix of savagery and passion, and I'm 100% here for it.

After a minute, he backs away to stand next to the bed, allowing my eyes to search out the other two. Both men stand at the end of the bed in all their naked, tatted glory. For a second, I think I might have cum just looking at these assholes. August is now dry. Now that I can see him fully, his body seems to scream a walking, talking piece of artwork. Dark lines cover every inch of his body. I knew he was tatted from the glimpses of skin here and there that I've seen, but I didn't expect this extent. The urge to paint him like Jack did Rose in the Titanic is strong. I wonder if he would pose for me. He smirks as I take in his lean, muscular form, almost like he knows where my mind went for a second. I suppose he could. He is my Picasso.

My eyes drift to Chase next, my Lover Boy. Where August is more classic artsy, Chase is an all-American boy next door with a dark secret. His tattoos cover his chest and arms, arranged in an array of colors. He is fit, toned and has the lickable six-pack to match. Chase holds his monster cock in his hand, long, thick and veiny as he slowly pumps himself in a loose hold. He stares down at me, eyes bright and alight with lust as he glides his tongue across his lips, as if trying to still taste me.

Dante steps up next to them, now fully naked as well. When we first hooked up in the beach house, it wasn't as lit as it is now. I knew he was pierced; I felt the cool metal when he entered me and when it hit that perfect spot inside, but seeing him like this is something else. His skin has a more olive complexion than the others and his whole demeanor screams bad boy, keep your daughters away. Which, of course, makes me even more turned on, like the sick bitch I am. Dante is my Lucifer, the devil. I have a feeling this man could talk me into selling my soul if he wanted.

"So how are we doing this, brother? Both of you have already been inside of her, so I call pussy dibs." Chase, ever so charming, says as he rubs his hands together in excitement.

"You can't call dibs like that, you idiot." August claims as his eyes zone in on said pussy. *What is taking these men so long?* I am in need, completely naked and bare to them, but they want to argue over who gets what hole. Fuck them.

I'll just make myself cum while the boys debate who gets to do what. Biting my lips, I glide my hands down my body. It's nothing like how they touch me, but my body is so on edge, any touch feels good. My fingers find my core as I massage my clit in sharp, tight circles, a moan slipping free, pulling the boys' attention to where my finger reaches for my opening. My other hand not occupying my core grips my breast, my fingers rolling my nipple into a stiff peak. I'm so sensitive from August and Chase earlier that it doesn't take longer before a climax builds. "Oh god, oh god." My back arches as my pussy spasms around my fingers before the bed dips around me.

A hand wraps around my throat, applying light pressure, making me snap my eyes open. Shit, I didn't even realize I closed them. Steel-gray eyes glare down at me. "You made your point, Cupcake, but there is no god, here. Only Heathens. Now on your knees and spread your thighs, I need to prep you."

I do as he says and scramble to my hands and knees. Chase slides beneath me and winks. "I called dibs on that perfect pink pussy of yours. So, climb aboard Kitten. It's time to make you purr." I want to laugh, but some twisted part of me finds his words hot.

I straddle Chase's wide hips as he places his cock at the opening of my core before sliding down until my hips meet his. He holds me in place for a minute to get used to his size as a finger traces down my spine until it reaches my ass. A second later, a palm lands on my ass. The sound of a quick slap followed by a sharp sting has me grinding down on Chase beneath me. "Fuck, D. She likes that. Do it again." A second spank landing on the opposite cheek has me arching my back, my core strangling Chase's cock. "Fuckkkkkk... Squeeze Kitten. That's it. Dante, man, prep this woman. I will not last if you keep this up. Her pussy is so fucking tight."

"My pleasure." Cool liquid is poured onto my ass before fingers start to probe my asshole. Another shift in the bed catches my attention as my head snaps in August's direction.

"Let me get your mind off D, Little Muse." August growls behind me, but I nod as he approaches, one hand reaching for my head and the other pumping his tatted cock in my face. I lick my lips in eager delight, making him chuckle. "I knew you were perfect for us. Greedy for each of us. You have Chase in your pretty pink pussy. Dante's about to claim that perky little ass, and you still want more." I nod, biting my lip. I have no intention of lying to the man. I crave to have every one of them. It would be great if they could destroy me in the best way possible. "Of course you do. You were made for us. Now open that sassy little mouth and suck me down until you gag." His words do naughty things to me, making both men already in me groan out as my body reacts. I do what he says, opening my mouth wide and relaxing my throat as he feeds me his rock-hard cock. I salivate around him as he hits the back, but I don't gag. He curses as he slides back just an inch before slamming forward, making my eyes water at the force.

I can feel my ass being stretched by Dante. He must have thought I was ready because the head of his thick cock presses in. I tense slightly before I remember that I need to relax, knowing once he is settled, it will be divine. Chase doesn't move beneath me, allowing Dante the room to fill me, but not wanting to feel left out, he leans up, sucking my nipple into his mouth. The sensations are incredible. It's like each guy knows which button to press to get a reaction out of me. If I were an instrument, these men would be prodigies, because the way they work together playing my body is like they have been playing it for years.

"That's a good girl. You have all three of us in you now. Are you ready?" August brushes the side of my face, cock still shoved down my throat. I look up at him with watery eyes full of desire and a challenge. He sees it. It's a dare to give me everything they got. That I'm ready. "Oh, Trinity. You won't be able to walk by the time we're done with you. Hang on, baby." A second later, I'm screaming around his cock as Dante pulls out and slams back into me. Chase following the cue. They take a second to find a rhythm, but when they do, I'm already a boneless mess of pleasure. I've never been so full in my life as Dante grips my hips, more than likely, leaving bruised imprints. Chase nips and sucks on my nipples, and August gripping my hair as he fucks my throat raw.

My moans mix with their groans, and curses as my climax hits like a tidal wave. I scream around August, making my throat tighten around his cock. It must have been too much because a second later he's slamming so far back into my throat that I choke, gasping for air I can't take. Jets of hot cum spray my throat, adding an odd, soothing sensation as I swallow him down. He pulls out, allowing my first deep breath before I'm licking my lips, savoring his taste on my tongue. "Good girl. Such a good fucking girl, swallowing me all down like that." I preen at his praise, arching my back, so Dante can hit deeper. "Do you want to cum now, Little Muse?"

CHAPTER TWENTY-ONE

DANTE

I watch as Trinity arches her back, giving me a better position to go deeper. My hands on her hips are tight, I'm sure, leaving bruises. The thought of leaving a mark on her fills my chest with satisfaction. Mine and Chase's pace don't stall as August finishes down Trinity's throat. Her moans are music to my ears as he praises her like the kitten Chase calls her. She preens at being called a good girl. She has a praise kink, for sure.

"Do you want to cum now, Little Muse?" August looks up at me with a smirk before he shifts down the bed towards me. I eye him as I continue my brutal pace. Her ass is so tight that I know I won't last much longer, so he better do what he plans to do now. He reaches under her body a second later, making her jerk at the sudden touch.

Chase curses. "Fuck, fuck, fuck, squeeze Kitten. Strangle my cock like you mean it." I feel her tighten around us, causing me to grind my teeth to not cum myself. "That's it baby, cum with me. Cum now!" As if waiting for the command, Trinity's body tenses, throwing her head back before letting out a low moan of Chase's name. Chase does the same before slamming his hips up, giving himself one last thrust as he spills inside her. He stills beneath her. "I knew you would purr for me, Kitten." He looks behind her, making eyes contact with me. "Now, I need you to make D lose control." I grit my teeth as Trinity looks over her shoulder at me. Her eyes are heavy, ridden with desire and probably exhaustion, before she smirks at me.

"What do you say, Lucifer? Show me what you got!" The sneaky minx slides forward before impaling herself on my cock. Letting out a gasp, followed by a moan. This woman. I lean forward, wrapping my hand around her small throat, before yanking her back to my chest as I sit up. I keep our bodies connected as I plaster her to me. Sweat drips from both of us as I nod to Chase to move. He pouts but scoots out of the way. I keep a firm grip on her neck as my other hand reaches down to find her clit. I find the swollen nub before rolling it between my fingers, causing her to twitch in my hold.

"You said you didn't understand that, after tonight, you will become our queen. Let me explain it to you." She nods, letting out a whimper of need as I play with her sensitive nub, but don't move other than that. "It means that we belong to you and you to us. You are our woman now. If we see another man even look at you like he thinks he might have a chance, we will kill him and deliver you his cock as a gift. I understand you don't think we know you, but we do. You proved that tonight, so don't fight us on this. Try to run, we will hunt. There is no escaping us now. We didn't come here to find you, but we aren't leaving without you, either. So, do you understand what all this means?" she nods, but that's not good enough. I pause, my movements on her clit. "Use your words, Cupcake, or I pull out, and you won't get to cum a last time."

"Yes." she blurts, making me chuckle at the desperation I hear in that single word. I place my finger back on her nub and apply pressure. She must know I won't do more because she speaks up again. "Yes, I understand. I'm yours. All of yours and all of you are mine. Which means I will kill any woman who looks in your direction, just the same as you."

"I expect nothing less, Cupcake. Now scream for me." I pull out before thrusting deep again. Keeping my hand around her throat as she writhes under my savage pace as I pound into her from behind. I feel I'm getting close to coming as my balls draw up. I can feel Trinity tightening, her breaths coming in short pants, so I reach down and pinch her clit hard as I roar my release. Painting the inside of her walls with my cum. A twisted part of me wishing it was her pussy. Now that she is our woman, a mini version of her and one of us wouldn't be so bad.

I hold her against my chest for another minute, allowing her inner muscles to milk me of everything I have, before slowly lowering her to the bed. She turns in my hold as I slip free, giving me a sleepy smile. I lean down and kiss her softly. "You did so good tonight, Cupcake. Sleep now, baby. We will talk when you wake up." I watch as her eyes drift close and her breathing evens out.

I finally step back when August steps up with a warm, wet cloth. He gently spreads her legs, wiping her clean. She'll probably want another shower in the morning, but this will work for now. The three of us step back and stare down at the beauty sleeping peacefully in my bed. "Wasn't this the hottest sex you've ever had? Also, can someone please take a picture? Because I have a feeling when she wakes up, she won't be so..." He points to her laying splayed out like a naked goddess on my bed and I understand. "This. You know." He shrugs before coming in next to her. He molds his body against her back, and subconsciously, she snuggles back to sneak body warmth from Chase. I glare at the fuck who is butt ass naked in my bed. "Don't look at me like that, D. I saved you her front half. Plus, you snooze, you lose boys. Gotta enjoy this calm before the storm hits." He closes his eyes before shoving his nose into her hair and inhales. His body relaxes within minutes.

I look over to August, who just shrugs. "I'll be in my studio." He nods to my bed. "He has a point. She won't be all mellow and relaxed in the morning. So, you better enjoy it now." He turns and heads for his room down the hall. Letting out a sigh, I climb in next to Trinity. Once again, she shimmies her body closer, seeking my warmth. A second later, her head finds my chest, causing me to hold my breath in fear she might wake and realize what she is doing, but she doesn't. I release the breath I was holding and settle in. Wrapping my arm around her waist and hoping that when she wakes, she doesn't fight the inevitable relationship between the four of us.

CHAPTER TWENTY-TWO

TRINITY

God, why am I so freaking hot right now? I shift in bed, attempting to kick off my covers, when I realize I don't have any blankets on. In fact, I'm completely naked and pleasantly sore all over. The memories of the night before rush through my head like watching a movie on fast-forward.

The diner.

The guys walking Ali home.

The creepy guy and his disgusting comments.

The moment he hit me, and I fell to the ground.

The red haze taking over. My knife in the man's chest.

The blood covering my body with its warm embrace.

Then the guys were just there. August took me back to their place before helping me wash all the blood away. One thing leading to another. The shower leading to the bed as Chase laid me out like a sacrificial lamb and then the best damn sex of my life. That explains the sore muscles and throat.

I can feel living heaters on both sides of me. Slowly I peek open a single eye to get a better grasp on how fucked I am. Plastered to my front is an oh so sexy Lucifer, lightly snoring away. *Who knew the devil was so peaceful when asleep?* Glancing back over my shoulder, I spot my Lover Boy laid out on his stomach, his arm wrapped around my stomach. The second thing I notice is that both men are equally naked, so being a warm-blooded woman, I take my fill.

I knew bad boys were mainly my type, but I have experienced nothing like I did last night. The way these men controlled my body was something else. And the things they kept saying were things I've dreamed of hearing from someone, but now I'm terrified. How could they say I'm theirs? They don't know me. It was all a heat of the moment thing. It had to be. They saw me kill a man and wanted to protect me, thinking I was a victim, but they were wrong.

Panic causes my heart rate to pick up. *I need air. I need space. I need to get out of here.* Both men are tangled up in my body, so it takes a bit of wiggling, but I maneuver myself far enough down to place Chase's arm around Dante's chest and Dante's leg up on Chase's thigh. When either of them moves, I scoot the rest of the way down the bed. Turning around, I wish I had my camera because this is a picture-perfect moment. I would get endless entertainment if I had a picture of them together like this. Knowing they will probably be pissed when they realize it's not a naked woman but a naked man they are cuddling, I scoop up the first shirt I see on the ground. Fresh pine fills my nose as I slip the gray cotton t-shirt over my head. The hem hits my upper thigh but will cover enough for the few feet it takes to get home. Without another glance, I head for the door that leads to the hall.

I've been in this house before, so I know the basic layout as I head for the front door. I barely reach the second door from the room I was just in when I hear the soft murmur of music coming from the room to my right. *Do you know the saying, curiosity killed the cat? I'm really surprised I'm still alive at this age.* Not being able to help myself, I step towards the room, a soft light emitting from the crack. I keep my footsteps light, figuring this is where August is, and I don't need him stopping me right now. Peeking through the crack in the door, I blink a couple of times. I must still be half asleep because the room looks like my garage. An art studio, but the part of the room I can see is filled with paintings of me.

As if in a trance, I stumble forward; the door creaking open. That's when I spot August in the corner, standing in front of an easel. He glances over his shoulder, his eyes giving me a once over. "I figured you'd be the first one up. You hungry?" My eyes jump to the canvas behind him and back. I nod dumbly as he sets down his brush before coming towards me. Once he is standing next to me, he turns back to the canvas, admiring his work. This piece is beyond what I expected. It's an enormous picture of me laid out on a sheet, bare for all to see. Shadows surround me as three sets of hands reach for my body, but not in scary monsters under the bed kind of way. From the look he painted on my face, it's a sexual way. Like I'm craving, begging, and pleading for these shadows to touch me. I can feel the passion bleeding from the canvas, and it's breathtaking.

"Why?" It's the only thing I can say as my eyes drift around the room. Canvas after canvas are images of me. Different colors, different positions, different art styles. August turns to me, then reaches up to cup my face. There's a moment that I think about pulling away from his touch, but I don't. The warmth of his palm covers my cheek, making me cringe.

"If you hadn't killed that bastard last night, I would have. I would have skinned him alive, bled him dry, and then used his blood as paint. He laid a hand on you, left a mark. He is lucky you got to him first." I shake my hand.

"Th-that's not what I asked. Why-" I look around the room. "Why all this?"

He stares into my eyes, searching for something before he leans in, brushing his plump lips against mine in a sweet, tender kiss. "Since the moment I saw you, I knew you were going to be ours. I felt lost with my art until I saw your eyes. It wasn't until you knocked on our door and shoved a plate of cookies at my chest that I painted anything real. That's when I knew I had my new muse. You." He whispers this against my lips before grabbing my hand, tugging me towards the door. "Now I make a mean omelet. Once the other two smell the food, they'll wake up and find us." He sends me a wink over his shoulder. "Then we have things we need to talk about." I nod in understanding, still reeling over the things he just said as we get to the kitchen. He leads me to a bar stool, nodding for me to sit before heading straight for a coffee machine in the corner. He pulls down a cup from the cupboard above, then goes to the fridge, grabbing creamer.

While the coffee brews, he turns, crossing his arms and leans against the counter. He's in a pair of low hung sweats and nothing else. I didn't notice all the bare skin covered in paint earlier, but I notice it now. "Actually, how does pancakes sound? I sort of have a sweet tooth after last night." His eyes dart down as if he could see my bare pussy behind the counter, licking his lips like he can still taste me. My cheeks blush with heat. How the hell could I still be ready for more play time when I lost count of how many times they made me cum? My pussy is a hussy, that's why.

I hop down from the stool. "Ummm, yeah. I can help. Gran taught me her recipe." Plus, anything to distract me from begging you to throw me over this counter to relive this damn heat would be great. Not that I say that second part, but from the smirk he gives me as he nods, I think he knows where my mind went.

I glance back towards the front door. If I ran now, I could make it? But I wouldn't get far. I have a feeling they will come for me. I suppose if I stay here, I won't have to hear Gran going on and on about how this exact scene happened in her damn porno book and that I just need to accept it. Yeah, I'll pass.

CHAPTER TWENTY-THREE

AUGUST

W atching Trinity waltz around the kitchen in a baggy t-shirt, creamy thighs on full display, is something else. She wasted no time gathering the ingredients and getting to work. I think she is still processing everything that happened last night, which makes sense. We all skipped the first date and told her she was ours now. She probably thinks it was just some manly expression, but we were dead serious. She is ours now, regardless of whether she thinks differently.

We don't talk as she flips another pancake, adding it to the already growing pile, but we continue to exchange small glances as we wait for the others to wake. Knowing this will be a long morning, I head to the coffeemaker to grab another cup when I hear Dante and Chase yelling at each other from down the hall.

"What the fuck do you think you're doing?!" There's a loud thump, like someone might have fallen out of bed, followed by pounding footsteps coming towards the kitchen.

"Looks like someone woke up on the wrong side of the bed." I mumble under my breath, making Trinity giggle.

"August! Where is she?" Dante calls out, but I don't answer. He will figure it out in a second. Sure enough, Dante rounds the corner wearing only boxers as his eyes immediately seek our woman. His body instantly relaxes when he spots her standing in front of the stove. He narrows his eyes at her. "Why didn't you wake one of us when you got up?" He questions, annoyed.

Before she can answer, Chase can be heard shuffling down the hall. "D, I wasn't reaching for your dick. I was reaching for Kitten's kitty cat. It's not my fault you were all cuddled close with morning wood. You were the one rubbing my thigh." He turns the corner before spotting all of us. "Oh. Awkward. Do you think they saw us?" He whispers shouts, making D lunge for him. Chase races forward to hide behind Trinity, causing D to pull up short, so he doesn't run our girl over like a bulldozer.

She turns, cocking a brow at him. "Oh, I saw everything. The second I scooted off, you two were two peas in a pod with each other. You're lucky I didn't have my camera, or I would have documented the entire thing." She holds up the plate of pancakes. "I made pancakes.

Gran's recipe. I say we eat, then exchange information. Yeah?" She looks at each of us one by one. We all nod before she nods, then sets the plate on the counter.

We don't bother with the kitchen table, each grabbing a plate and a few pancakes to eat where we stand. Trinity grabs her plate and a cup of coffee before having a seat at the breakfast nook. We eat in silence until everyone is done. I collect everyone's dishes, placing them in the sink to wash later. I would typically clean now, but this conversation is more important.

"Soooooo, who wants to start?" Trinity eyes each of us, crossing her arms over her chest in a clear statement that she is not volunteering. I eye the other two. We haven't had a chance to talk about how we wanted to approach this topic with her. When no one says anything right away, Trinity speaks again. "Okay, what about the body?"

"What about it?" Dante asks gruffly, mimicking her by crossing his arms over his chest, then leans back against the counter.

"Look, I remember what happened last night. I'm guessing you guys did something with the body, since I woke up naked in a man sandwich and not in handcuffs. I'm asking if I should pack to run or not."

"No." Is Dante's only reply. I swear, the asshole is a caveman. The next thing we know, he is going to bring out a club and bang against his chest.

"What Dante means is no; you don't have to worry about the body. We took care of it." Instead of relaxing at the thought, Trinity narrows her eyes.

"Why?" She holds up a hand. "Don't 'why what' me! Why didn't you call the police or something? You all acted like it was nothing seeing your next-door neighbor covered in blood, stabbing a man to death."

This time, we all just shrug. It was nothing to us. Granted, it's usually us covered in blood, not a woman we all want, but tomato, tomato. "Can I just say something?" Chase leans forward to look Trinity in the eye. "I thought it was hot as fuck. I'm getting hard just thinking about it. Ouch!" I slap the back of his head. "What was that for? You both were thinking it, too."

"Why didn't you guys freak out?" I can hear the suspicion in her tone.

"Simple Cupcake. We're killers. We do this for a living." She stares at us for a minute before breaking out in a ruckus laughter. I eye the others, a little concerned by her reaction, thinking we might have broken her. She murmurs under her breath as her laughter finally dies down.

"I knew it. I knew I was unhinged. Why wouldn't I fall for killers? I'm a killer. I knew I was. I enjoyed it the first time, but I thought I could fight it. But nooooo... I had to be a freak and crave the way it felt to kill someone." Her eyes snap up, widening as she continues her rant. "He had it coming. It was me or him. I knew that. I was just laying there. He had beaten me pretty badly that night, but I knew that was the night he wasn't going to stop. There was so much madness in him; he was drunk and so angry. Then he found mom with someone else in bed again. He started going on and on about how it was my fault. Everything was my fault. He killed her first. There was so much blood, I tried to save her. I ran at him, knocking him over, but he was always bigger and stronger than me. He hit me, and I was dazed, but something happened to me while I was laying there waiting for him to kill me. Everything went red. I couldn't stop even if I wanted to, but I didn't want to. He deserved it all." She takes a shaky breath, taking a second to calm herself. "Gran found me. I was covered in my dad's blood. She knew he was an abusive bastard. Gran is my mother's mom. I wasn't crazy or insane to her. She understood. She helped me make it look like he killed my mother, beat me until he thought I was dead, and then jumped off the cliffs. Murder suicide. The cops here didn't care to look into it. It would have been too much paperwork if they had. So they wrote it off, and I was sent to live with Gran." She didn't shed a single tear explaining that to us, which only makes her more perfect for us.

"Shit, Kitten, you're a badass bitch. Is it too early to ask you to marry me?" She rolls her eyes. "Fine, we can talk more about that later. I guess it's only fair to explain why we are here now." She shrugs.

"I'm going to take a wild guess and say it has something to do with the missing girls and the mayor." My eyes snap to the guys in shock. I think we assumed she might know something, but that just summed it up. She notices our shocked expressions and giggles. "I figured. The guy last night. I think he was after Ali. I think I recognized his voice. One night, I saw something and took some pictures. They're dark, but you can clearly see the mayor and another guy shove a girl into the trunk."

"Why didn't you go to the police and report it?" I ask, curious. Most women go running to law enforcement. She laughs in my face at my question.

"The chief and mayor are close friends. Look, can I head home to shower and dress? I can show you the pictures, and I need to check on Gran."

Dante gives her a smirk as he stands straight. "Yeah Cupcake. Gran invited us over for lunch anyway." She goes to object, but he steps into her space and grips her chin, making her look up at him. "We told you last night you were ours. Now be a good girl and allow us a second to grab you sweats and for us to get dressed. If you want to argue, I'll bend you over this counter right now and remind you of what you agreed to last night."

She visibly gulps before she straightens her shoulders, placing a palm on D's chest, and pushes him back.

"Listen here Lucifer. I said I remember everything that happened last night. You said I was now yours, but you also said I was your queen. If you don't mind your tongue, I might get a little stabby again."

"You don't scare me, Cupcake. I like a little pain, plus I could take you." He licks his lips in a taunting manner, and I see the exact moment Trinity's demeanor changes. I wince as she reaches forward, lightening fast, and grabs a handful of Dante's junk. He cringes but remains standing. Brave fucker. Brave, but such an idiot.

"I never said what I would be stabbing. But I think a better punishment would be you having to watch as I ride August and Chase over and over and over. Never once allowing you to touch me. Wouldn't that be fun? How long could you go without me getting on my knees for you, Dante?" A second later, she slams her mouth down on his, making him react. Dante grabs the back of her head and I watch as they basically dry hump each other. I finally clear my throat, making them pull away. "Don't make me punish you, Lucifer. You wouldn't like it. Now, go get ready. Gran must be worried about me."

Chase shoves his hand into his pants and readjusts himself. "Fuck, that was hot. Can I be next?"

Same brother, same.

CHAPTER TWENTY-FOUR

TRINITY

I t doesn't take the guys long to get dressed and within minutes; we are headed back to my place. Since I misplaced my bag, I knocked once at the front door. I hadn't checked the time, but the sun is up and knowing Gran, so is she. She answers quickly, giving me a wide grin as she takes me and the guys in. I squeeze in between her and the door frame, wanting to get to my room to shower as quickly as possible. I need a bit of space to decompress and go over everything that has happened in the last 24 hours. As I'm passing Gran, she whispers, "I told you would end up with them. Your very own harem. How exciting." I don't bother rebutting her statement, knowing she probably noticed I didn't come home. I'm not in my own clothes, and I'm pretty sure I have the well known after sex glow.

"I'm going to go shower and change. Then we will finish talking." I say over my shoulder. Making a B line to my room.

"I'll start the coffee and whip up some food." Gran heads to the kitchen as the guys follow.

"I can come wash your back for you, Kitten." Chase calls out.

"I'm perfectly capable. Maybe next time." I roll my eyes but smile to myself. Somehow, these guys have made it past my walls and I haven't decided how I really feel about it yet.

"I'm holding you to that." He yells out as I enter my bedroom, locking the door behind me.

I lean my back against the door, taking a few seconds for myself to just breathe. These guys are a lot and are making me feel weird. No one has ever cared about me other than Gran and then, suddenly, I have three guys saying I'm theirs and hiding a dead body for me. It's actually kind of romantic in some dark, twisted, fairy tale kind of way.

After a few minutes of calming breaths, I finally drag my ass to the bathroom. Flipping on the handle, I turn the water to boiling because I'm a woman, and we are from the fires of hell. I strip off my borrowed clothes, taking half a second to inhale the fresh pine scent of Chase before stepping under the spray. I allow the hot water to soothe my achy muscles as the activities of the night before flashes through my head. August's hands on my body, washing the blood down the drain before devouring me whole. I swear I saw actual stars as he brought me to climax. Then realizing Chase and Dante were watching as August fucked me against the shower wall. And the bed. Oh, god. Those men knew what they were doing. My body tingles at the memories, and I have to force myself to think about anything but the guys. I go through the motions of washing my hair and body, making double sure all the evidence is washed away.

I have a feeling that last night isn't the last time I'll have to deal with an asshole trying to have what doesn't belong to him. Plus, I think the guys have a lot of information on what is going on around here as well. As I finish up my shower, I wrap a towel around my body, feeling more like myself. I stand in front of the mirror and see a big, nasty bruise on my right cheek. I narrow in on it, cursing myself. Should have just stabbed first and asked questions later, but I've always tried to hide my crazy. I didn't need anyone looking at me closer to realize I was far from sane. Oh well, a little makeup will cover that right up, or maybe I can say I ran into a door or something.

Deciding to deal with that later. I head for my room to find I'm not alone anymore. Dante is standing at my desk in the corner, flipping through my sketchbook.

Shit. "What are you doing here? Wait, I locked the door. How did you get in?" He doesn't answer, just continues to stare down at my doodles.

"I thought you hated me, but this doesn't scream hate." He holds up the sketch book opened to a page of sketches of his face from every angle. At the time, I thought if I drew him, I could get him out of my head. It didn't work. I thought about him more, and every night he and the guys showed up for dinner.

"It's nothing but bored doodling. I needed something interesting to draw, and there you were. Don't overthink it." I head to my dresser, ignoring the way his eyes follow my every move. "Now can you leave so I can get dressed? I'll be out in a few minutes so we can all chat." He doesn't respond, but I hear him set the notebook down, followed by a scuffle of footsteps but not towards the door.

Dante presses into my back, his warmth filling me with an odd sense of safety. "I've already seen you naked and laid out on my bed. I've tasted your sweet juices, felt you cum around my cock, so don't be shy now." He grabs the edge of my towel and yanks. The fabric falling to the ground, leaving me once more bare to this man. His hands find my hips, spinning me to face him. "I know what is going through your mind. You think last night was all a ploy to get you into our beds, but it wasn't. You have a dark side Cupcake.

We saw it last night." I go to shake my head, but he grips my chin, pausing my movements. "I won't lie to you. Before last night, I wanted to just fuck you. You intrigued me and not a lot of women can do that, but when I saw you straddling that man, covered head to toe in his blood... I knew." He leans down, making us eye level, his lips grazing mine. "I knew you were made for us." His lips slam down on me, devouring me, and I don't have the strength to fight it. Hands suddenly grip under my ass and lift me before Dante moves. A second later, I'm set on my bed. Not once does Dante break the kiss.

"What are you doing, Lucifer?" I'm panting as his kisses drift down my neck, over my collarbone and between my breasts.

"I'm not just the big bad guy you want me to be. I can be whatever you need. We all can. Let me show you." He stares up at me from between my legs. I didn't even realize my legs opened automatically for him. His eyes are pleading, and who am I to deny this man? Especially if I think I know where this is going. I give him the tiniest of head nods, but it's enough because a moment later he sends me a grin before diving in. Dante gets to work, claiming his nickname of Lucifer as his tongue does its magic. "Hush Cupcake. You don't want everyone to hear you." I bite my lip to not cry out as Dante's fingers join in the mix. "That's it, squeeze my fingers, baby." A small moan slips past my lips. "Good girl. The faster you cum, the faster we can all talk. I want you to cum. Now." He shoves his fingers deep into my core, hitting that one spot before nipping at my clit. My entire body tenses, back arching, toes curling as a climax rolls through me. Dante drinks in my juices as I come down from my euphoric high, sitting back on his heels as he wipes his mouth clean. "I'm sorry, Cupcake, but you can't leave us now. You'll understand when we explain why we are here. Now get dressed."

I sit up on my arms, cocking a brow. "Is that how you apologize to women?" He smirks, but shakes his head.

"I don't apologize to anyone." He turns and heads for the door.

"That sure seemed like an, I'm sorry for being an asshole to you, apology."

"Maybe you're just special, Cupcake." Sending me a wink over his shoulder, he leaves my room. The moment the door clicks shut, I throw myself back into the mattress.

Ugh. Why are these men so complicated? I want to not like them, but their looks and personalities are everything I wanted in a guy. Each gives me something different. And the sex. God, the sex is beyond what I could have ever wanted. Which all means one thing. Gran was right. I need these guys in my life, but if they say I'm theirs, they better believe they are mine. Maybe I should make that clear.

I quickly slip into a pair of black leggings and a simple white t-shirt, then gather my hair into a casual, messy bun. Since everyone in the house has already seen my face, I skip the concealer altogether. I add a pair of fuzzy socks for comfort, then head out to find the guys. I make a beeline for the kitchen, confident that's where Gran would be. Sure enough, she is standing at the counter stirring what looks like a cookie mix. She must hear me enter because she spins around quickly, opening her arms wide for an embrace. I waste no time rushing into her wide-open arms as they envelop me with unconditional love. "It happened again, Gran. The red haze came, and I couldn't stop it." She holds me tighter in understanding.

"I know Sweetheart. I helped the boys clean up the mess. This isn't our first killing, and I don't think it will be your last." I look at her wide-eyed. Does she really think that? That I'll just keep going around killing people? I want to protest, express my anger and rage, but she hushes me with a hand covering my mouth. "Oh, hush, child. There is nothing wrong with that. It does not change the fact that you are my grandchild and I love you so. I won't be here forever, and I need to make sure you have someone to stand by your side. Those boys will do just that. They didn't hesitate for a second to take care of you last night." She paused, giving me a devious smile. "And by the looks of you, they took care of you real good. You are practically glowing right now."

"Gran!" I gasp. This woman has one of the dirtiest minds I know. I swear, if I wasn't her flesh and blood, she might have asked me for a play-by-play.

"Don't pretend like nothing happened. I was right about those boys, wasn't I?" She cocks her brow at me, but I look away. My non answer is enough as Gran beams before turning back to her bowl of dough. "Now I'm going to pop these in the oven. I made some sandwiches and put them in the living room with the boys. Now go on and take the tray of drinks with you. I'll be there shortly." With nothing else to say, I grab the tray of drinks she made and head to the living room. I can hear the lower murmurs of my guys as I enter the doorway, catching their attention as they go quiet.

"Secrets don't make friends, boys." I tsk at them, setting the tray down on the coffee table. I grab a coffee and head straight for Chase. He looks a little shocked as I approach, but once I'm directly in front of him, I give him my back, then plop down in his lap. I manage to not spill a single drop of golden goodness as I snuggle in. Chase's arms wrap around my body after his initial shock wears off, leaning in to mold my body to his. I hear him take a deep inhale, running his nose up my neck to my ear before nipping, causing me to giggle.

"Soooo, you accept us then?" August asks, sitting across from us. I look towards him as he eyes me with desire. Turning my gaze to where Dante stands, I see he is watching me with just as much heat as well.

"I'll let you know for sure once you give me more information. As of now, I don't want to kill you. Does that work?" Bringing my coffee cup to my mouth, I blow gently, cooling it off a little before taking a small sip. Dante moves to take a seat, and I turn in Chase's lap to face him.

"Well, you already know we are killers. They call us the Heathens."

CHAPTER TWENTY-FIVE

CHASE

To say I was shocked that Kitten walked her sexy little ass right up to me and plopped down on my dick was, to say the least. If this wasn't a claiming move, I don't know what is. Women do that right, drape themselves over a man to show ownership. I honestly thought we were going to have to fuck her senseless a few more times before maybe taking her to Vegas to get drunk married. *Wouldn't that be a sight?* She might try to kill us after, but we would be legally married and that's all that mattered, because she couldn't leave us after that.

Dante continues to explain everything as I try to think about anything other than Kitten's tight body snuggled up against mine; like singing the ABC's backwards. Z...Y...X...W... "We work for a man who does bad things. The boss has his hands in many pies, but he still holds a certain code. He deals in mostly drugs, guns, and underground shit like gambling and fighting, but he has a strict policy about skins." He pauses for a second, probably trying to figure out how to explain all this. "I suppose I should start by why we are here." She nods, not speaking but listening intently. "Like I said, our boss doesn't deal in skins. If he even thinks someone who works for him is thinking about trafficking skins, he cuts all ties." He gives her a look, saying it's not a friendly breakup. "That's where we come in."

"So you're, what, contract killers?" Trinity looks at each of us, but none of us rebuts the statement. "Ugh, why are all the hot ones the crazy dangerous ones too?" She slumps back against my chest, making me feel all warm and fuzzy.

"In a sense, yes. We get sent in to take care of the problem, but not before we investigate the claims fully. Our boss doesn't just give us names to take out. He wants proof before we do. Sometimes it's a rival spreading rumors, knowing who their boss is. When the claims ring true, which is not always the case, we make an example of them." I explain, inhaling her sweet sugary scent again. I'm aware that it's creepy, but there's something about the scent of her that is incredibly alluring. I'm basically a Kitten addict at this point. If I don't get my fix on a regular basis, I'm not sure what I will do.

"Yes, like Chase said, we investigate the claim before any killing happens. Our boss has been using this town as a middle point. Things get shipped to and from the port. The mayor is the main point of contact for this area, and rumor is he's gotten into the skin trade." Kitten nods as if agreeing with D.

"Our research shows an increase in missing girls between the ages of thirteen and twenty-five. All from the surrounding towns and states. Our boss has heard rumors that his ports were being used as a drop-off point for the missing girls, and that the mayor knows all about it. We know the guy is shady but have found nothing 100% concrete; but after last night, I think it's safe to say shit is going down. We just need to figure out who." August explains. Kitten doesn't seem all that surprised by the news.

"The mayor is involved, I can tell you that. I also think the chief of police and a few others as well. Last night, I think they were after Ali. Our boss Chad is a sleaze ball and asked her to stay late to close. On her own." She looks around the room, taking a deep breath and fiddling with her fingers. "The guy I killed last night, he was at the diner right before you guys came in. He was creepy and kept asking Ali out for drinks or asking when she was getting off. We get creeps in all the time. It comes with being a young woman in a small town, but he was different. He also sounded familiar." Kitten goes to stand, but I tighten my arms around her. "Let me up, Lover Boy. I have evidence you will want." I give her a pout before surging in for a quick kiss, which she returns. She rushes from the room the second I release her. Turning to my brothers, giving them a smug smile because she chose me.

Before they can complain, or I can gloat, Gran enters the room with a plate of freshly baked, still warm, chocolate chip cookies. This woman is a saint, but before I can break her heart by telling her I can't marry her because my heart belongs to her granddaughter, Kitten returns. I wait for her to return to my lap, but frown when she heads for Dante's. Instead of plopping down, D scoops her up and cradles her in his lap like he is holding a fine China and is afraid it might break if he moves. I go to protest my disapproval that she is no longer in my lap when she holds up a handful of photos.

August goes to grab the stack while I reach for the cookies. I lean back in my seat and wait until August passes me the photos, all the while watching as D's thumb rubs small circles against Trinity's thighs. "You saw this happen?" August looks stunned as he inspects the pictures, then turns to the woman in question. He passes me the pictures and I flip through them quickly. Images of a man grabbing a woman from behind as she struggles. Another man steps out of the nice-looking car to pop open the trunk. The pictures were taken at night, but with a streetlamp nearby, you can clearly see the shape of the men's profile.

"The man last night. I think he is the second guy in the photos. The other is definitely the mayor. I've lived in this town long enough to know that." Trinity leans against D's chest, and I watch as the unfeeling bastard actually let out a small genuine smile.

"Why didn't you tell us last night?" That's the real question. We could have helped her. Prevented all of last night from happening and had a nice movie night date with junk food, beer, and cuddles. But then would the hot sex have happened after?

Maybe it should have played out the way it did. That's how we got here, isn't it?

"I didn't know for sure. Plus, Ali can't take care of herself like I can. I knew there was a chance he would still go after her, but figured he would think I was an easy target as well. It worked out in the end; Ali is safe, and the asshole is dead."

"Speaking of, did he say anything last night?" August asks, grabbing a cookie as he takes his seat again. We watch as Trinity replays the night before in her head. Her eyes seemed to glaze over for a minute.

"Well, he had mentioned the disgusting things he wanted to do to me. How I ruined his easy night but that I would do just fine." She tilts her head to the side as a cute little frown appears on her lips. "He mentioned the carnival."

"Carnival?" I ask. "Is that like a secret phrase or a sex club?"

Everyone looks at Betty as she explains. "The Halloween carnival. The mayor makes a big deal out of it every year. Rides, vendors, entertainment, he even has a fun house. All the neighboring towns come as well. They won't let you in unless you are dressed up."

"He said something about after the carnival they would ship me off." She perks up suddenly. "Does that mean the girls they have taken so far we can save them?" She gives us all hopeful eyes.

"In theory, we need more details. Do they move the girls somewhere? Are they bringing in the girls from somewhere? Who is the mayor working with? How many people are involved? There are still too many variables." August explains as Kitten gets this determined glint in her eye.

Trinity jumps up from D's lap, making him grunt and reach for her. Ha bastard, how does it feel? She steps away and faces the room. "I want to help. What if I was bait or something?"

As if we were one person, a resonating "No!" echoes off the walls.

Chapter Twenty-Six

Trinity

I cross my arms over my chest and glare at the three assholes sitting in the room who think they can tell me what I can and can't do. "I wasn't asking."

"Yes, you were." I snap my glare at Lover Boy. They don't get real names until they can stop being overbearing, typical men.

"Well, I'm not anymore. Either you let me help you guys or I do it on my own. Your choice." I give them my best award-winning white smile as I cross my arms over my chest.

"Boys. I would let her help if I were you. This girl is as stubborn as they come, and I know she will go off on her own if you don't let her help. I would hate to see something bad happen to my grandbaby all because of your egos and overzealous mindset that women can't be useful." Gran comes to my defense, making me grin impossibly wider. The woman knows me so well.

"Betty, that's not what we are saying. It's dangerous what we do and we don't want to see anything happen to Trinity." August takes a step forward, holding out his hand in a non-defensive way, but halts as my grin shifts to a mischievous smile.

I turn to Dante, cocking a brow in question. "Didn't you say I was your guy's queen?"

"Not when it comes to putting yourself in danger. Cupcake, we have been doing this for a while. The guys we deal with aren't just assholes and scumbags. We don't even know who the mayor is sending the girls to. We don't have enough information about the situation. He could have an army of men helping him and we only have a week to figure this all out before the next exchange. We can't be worrying about you while trying to stop this asshole." Dante's eyes are hard, but I can see the worry in them. While August's eyes are screaming to please understand. Chase just shoves another cookie in his mouth before sending me a blue-eyed wink.

I let my shoulders slump while my eyes dart to the floor. Dropping my arms as well. "You're right. It's too dangerous. I won't get involved." Letting out a deep exhale in defeat, the guys all give me a satisfied look and a head nod. I turn to head back to my room to pout about my loss in this argument, but before I could even take a step away, Gran laughs. Damn it. My eyes dart back up to the woman in question who is now holding her stomach, slapping her knee in an over exaggerated display of laughter.

"Betty! What's wrong? Are you okay? Are you having a heart attack or something?" Chase rushes to her side, eyes wide with panic. The other two look mildly worried but aren't in a full freak out mode like their brother. Chase looks between all of us, trying to figure out what to do. The look on his handsome face almost causing me to laugh along with Gran. She finally takes in air, calming her over dramatic ridiculousness. She waves Chase away before chuckling again as she takes in the guys in the room.

"Are you alright Betty?" Dante asks, cocking a brow in her direction. I let out a long loud exhale, gathering everyone's attention, knowing Gran is about to throw me under a large metaphorical speeding bus. She gives me a bright smile, causing me to narrow mine at her in betrayal. So much for her having my back.

"Did you gentlemen really believe Trinity was just going to drop this whole thing?" She cocks a brow at them in question as they snap their eyes back in my direction. I shrug my shoulders, then roll my eyes at their disapproving looks. Can they blame me? "She didn't give you all the information yet." She shakes her head like I'm a troublesome child and not a capable young woman. "Trinity works for the newspaper occasionally. This year they asked her to cover the Halloween carnival. Take pictures for future advertisements and to show that our little town is such a lovely place to visit or live." This time she rolls her eyes, knowing this place is the worst. But now I know where I really get all my sass from. "She has to meet with the mayor beforehand to do a quick Halloween photoshoot. You know, to show how even the mayor gets into the holiday spirit. If I know my granddaughter like I do, she will find a way to look through his office." Giving me a wink, she adds. "It's what I would do if I were her."

Everyone is silent while they process Gran's words, making me feel a bit uncomfortable as the guy's faces twist from their concern for Gran to what might be anger that I was lying about dropping the topic. I throw my arms out and shrug. "What?! You didn't actually think I was going to just sit back and do nothing. They got me involved when that fucker from last night attacked me. They wanted my friend. And you didn't hear the disgusting and vile things that guy wanted to do to me. What he has probably done to many girls!" I'm yelling at this point, but I don't care. Rage is building in me, and it needs an outlet. "You all opened Pandora's box when you said you all wanted me." I throw my arms out to the side. "This is me, boys. Either let me help or I'll hunt the fucker myself and make him pay." Hands on my hips now, I stand there, chin held high and defiant.

These guys need to learn if they want me, then a whole lot of crazy comes with it. I never thought I would find someone who actually wanted me. Saw the ugly side and still thought I was perfect. I know these guys can be totally full of shit. They could be playing a game with me, like who could break Trinity first, but they saw me last night. They saw me covered in blood, with my knife in a man's chest. Shit, I even stabbed one of them, but they took me in, washed me, then showed me I wasn't alone. Their words, their hands, their kisses, all soft and tender, all claiming. I felt wanted for what felt like the first time in my life; other than Gran. Dante called me their queen. August has a room filled with paintings of me. And Chase, I think Chase is crazy enough to kidnap me and forge my signature on a marriage license. At this point, I'm not giving these men an option to leave me. Ever.

"That was beyond sexy as fuck. I bet you give the best angry sex?" Chase purrs in his usual flirty way.

"Shut up." Dante snaps before standing from his chair and heading towards me. I steel my spine, prepared for some more alphahole bullshit. It's not safe. This is a man's world. You could get hurt... Blah blah blah. What I don't expect is for the giant of a man to stop in front of me with a thin lip glare on his beautiful face before softening his features, then proceeding to kneel in front of me. I'm so shocked that I just stand there dumbfounded as I stare at him. The shuffling of clothes pulls my attention, making me look up to see August and Chase both approaching as well. Neither man glares like Lucifer but each takes a spot on either side of him and kneels as well. I stumble back a step with the intensity of each man's stare. I know what my brain was just saying about not giving these men an option and that they were stuck with me but shit. They are looking up at me like a stage 5 clinger hearing I'm leaving for work for the day. I suddenly don't feel so confident with my recent rant until Dante opens his pretty mouth. "You're right."

I blink in return. What is a woman supposed to say or do when she was readying her defenses for an argument and then bam, you're right. I mean, most women are right, most of the time and guys just can't accept it, but to hear them admit it... is just odd. I'm just at a loss for words and he must see it because he chuckles, reaching for my hand.

"You're right. You were involved the moment they sent someone after you. We're sorry for trying to keep you out of it. We just wanted to keep you safe, but I see that we have a lot to learn about each other, but we have time. I know this is all still new, but let's get one thing straight. You are right, you are our queen now." He tilts his head in a small bow. "But you're not going off by yourself to play. Let's make a plan together."

"As long as I can stab someone." I smile sweetly as all three men stand, Dante chuckling again before grabbing my waist and yanking me to his chest, lips grazing mine.

"You can stab as many assholes as you want, baby. You covered in our enemy's blood would be a beautiful sight." Then his lips are crashing down on mine in a rough but passionate kiss. I'm helpless as my body melts under his, heating to a feverish temperature. A second later I'm sucking in air as I'm spun, another pair of lips taking Dante's place. This kiss is more delicate but no less passionate. August, my sweet lover.

"Only you could have a Heathen kneel for you. Don't think you can get rid of us now." He whispers before I'm yanked to the side, falling into another hard chest.

"I want to make something very clear. I called dibs before those assholes." Chase's kiss is teasing, much like the man, as his lips nip at mine playfully. His blue eyes shine with desire as he licks the seam of my lips, asking for entrance.

The smell of popcorn fills my senses, causing me to pull away from my lover boy. My eyes find Gran sitting on the couch, eyes filled with joy. Sure enough, on her lap is a bowl of popcorn. The woman just shrugs before tossing a handful into her mouth and chews. When I continue to just stare at her, she shrugs. "What? It was just getting good." My mouth drops open as the guys all shake with contained laughter. "Also, this is just like in my books. The men say something stupid, upset the girl, then have to grovel for forgiveness. This is better than TV." She waves his frail hand in our direction. "Please continue." That makes the guys lose it as the room fills with loud, raucous laughter, making me smile. Gran sends me a wink as I shake my head.

I've always felt so alone until Gran took me in. Like I had to hide my real self; and I know it's fast, but now with these guys I think I can finally be myself and let the part of me I've kept hidden be free.

CHAPTER TWENTY-SEVEN

TRINITY

I t took me all week to get the guys to see the reason for my plan. They don't agree or even like it, but it's the only way. If we started asking questions, they could move the girls sooner or even go into hiding. I did some research about missing girls in the area, including surrounding states, and I've found at least fifteen that these guys could have taken. There were more missing girls recorded, but I'm hoping some were really just runaways. The fifteen or so are just the ones from recent weeks. The number would be much higher if I went further back in my search. I just don't understand how it seems like no one cares.

"I really don't like the idea of you being in the same room as this fucker. What if he recognizes you? You said the fucker who attacked you told you he informed his boss of the change. His disappearance is probably noticeable, too. What if they figure out you were his target and they try to take you again?" Dante sits at the edge of my bed as I towel dry my hair. I've lost count of the number of times he has tried to change my mind about the plan. When I explained I was doing the mayor's photoshoot at his office, Dante was adamant about finding a different way. He refused to see the fact that I would have the perfect chance to find information. What better way than from the source? The mayor would be too busy with his final arrangements and the Halloween carnival. He wouldn't notice little ole me.

Chase was all supportive, going on and on about the best way to sneak around and potential places to check for secret information. I swear, I think he thought we were in a spy movie or something. August was a bit more resigned, but saw my reasoning. This was the best chance we had at saving those girls. Dante is still a stone wall, in his opinion. I even tried to use my sexual wiles to persuade him to see my side of it.

"Lucifer, I know you are worried about me, but I can do this. I promise. I'll have you on speed dial if anything goes wrong. Then you can be my knight in dark amour and come save me." I give him a sexy smirk, an idea coming to mind. "I'll make you a deal." He cocks a brow in question. Still wrapped in a towel from my shower a minute ago, I placed myself between his widespread legs. Biting my lip in excitement, I lower myself to the ground in front of him, placing my hands on his thick thighs. "If you have to come save me, I'll be on my knees for you every day for a month." His steel-gray eyes flicker with desire for a second before he narrows them to my lips.

"Doing what?" He challenges.

"Would you like a quick demonstration?" I bite my lip in anticipation. I should get dressed right now. The Halloween carnival starts soon, and I need to do the stupid photoshoot for the mayor before, but a quick demo shouldn't take up too much time. Dante gives me a nod, but I'm already reaching for his pants. I rush through, flicking open the button, followed by the sound of the zipper being undone, before he lifts just enough for me to wiggle his jeans down. I waste no time reaching into his boxer shorts, gripping his cock, releasing it from its confines. He hisses as I tighten my grip before leaning forward and giving it a long lick from base to tip. His body shudders as I swirl my tongue around the tip. Deciding I have little time to enjoy this, I get to work. With no warning, I slam my mouth down around Dante's cock. Curses fill the air as I keep him there, keeping my mouth full before swallowing to tighten around him. His hands fly to my head, fingers wrapping around strands of my hair. I begin to bob, slowly at first, before saying fuck it and speeding up my pace. Dante attempts to contain my pace but fails, especially as I take him fully in without gagging. His piercing rubs against my throat almost in a tickle, but I stay focused. Reaching up, I grip his balls in one hand, gently rolling them around. That must do it because I hear a "Fuck! Fuck! Fuck!" before warm salty seed fills my mouth. I swallow down everything he gives before pulling back and smiling up at my Lucifer, who is now panting, slumped back against my bed.

"Fuck Cupcake. You have a deal." I giggle, getting to my feet.

"I figured, now get home. I gotta get dressed before heading to the photoshoot. You all need to stake out the carnival. I'll meet you out front." He sits up, tucking himself back into his pants before standing. His hand snaps out, grabbing my neck, pulling me to him, forcing my head to look up at him.

"The second you're unsure, you call. If something happens to you, I will hunt you down just to put you over my knee and turn that juicy little ass red. Then, when you're begging me to make you cum, I will deny you. Do you understand?" I nod, wide-eyed. *He wouldn't do that, would he?* "Use your words, Cupcake."

"Y-Yes, I understand." Shit, my voice came out shaky. His words combined with how going down on him made me horny. My body is on fire right now. Damn, planning a murder. It's getting in the way of me getting laid.

"Good girl." His lips lower to mine, but instead of a "give me your soul" kind of kiss, Dante kisses me gently with a "here is my heart, don't break it" kind of kiss. The kiss ends too quickly, but I know I'll have more soon. He leaves me to prepare with the costumes we picked out earlier this week. Excitement thrumming inside. I went over my mental checklist one last time.

Get in.

Get the information.

Get out.

Kill some assholes.

Save the girls.

Have amazing mind-blowing sex with three hot as sin men.

After Dante left, I could focus on getting ready for the night. We all went shopping for costumes earlier this week, and I was pretty excited about mine. I never got into the holiday spirit before now, so it was interesting finding an outfit. The guys were pretty easy since they decided to go wearing all black, with each of them having a different neon light - up face mask. I kinda thought it was hot as hell. For me, the guys came up with a sexy devil, naughty nurse, preppy cheerleader and even a pretty princess. I'm pretty sure they were naming off the most common and basic costumes out there. While I was browsing the shop, I stumbled upon the face painting section. There was an image of a little girl dressed as a skeleton with a full face. Then I got an idea. Day of the dead. In a way, I kind of matched the guys, choosing bright neon colors for my makeup.

To begin, I gently spread a thin layer of white make-up across my face and neck. I followed up with black lines outlining my lips, teeth, neck, cheekbones, and adding large circles around my eyes. Using neon colors, I brought my artwork to life with detailed designs and carefully applied shading. I curled my hair quickly and added a crown of colorful flowers last. My outfit was simple. I went with an all-black bodysuit that had the outline of skeleton bones on my body. The bodysuit clung to all my curves and had a low cut v-slit in the front so my chest was on full display. I decided to go with comfort over looks and went with a pair of all-black high-top converses. I saw my reflection and couldn't shake the feeling that I looked like myself, but with a wicked twist.

After I finished all that, I scooped up my backpack and headed out. I knew the guys were headed to the carnival a bit early to get the layout and maybe see if we can spot anything out of place. You know, like guards or a place, these girls might be stored. I was to meet them out front once I was done at the mayor's office.

I took Gran's car so that it's easier to get back to the carnival or make a quick getaway. Once there, I headstraight for his office.

His office was located in the town hall building on main street. As I approached the door at the end of the hall, I expect to see a secretary or something, but no one is there to greet me. I wait for a minute, thinking maybe they went to the restroom or to print papers or whatever secretaries do but no one shows. I hear raised voices through the cracked door, my curiosity gets the best of me. *It would have been ironic if I dressed as a cat.*

I pull out my phone when I overhear a man's voice says *carnival*. I keep my footsteps light as I approach, just like Chase taught me. Opening the recording app on my phone, I peek into the room. Not much could be seen since the door's just barely cracked open, but I could still see the mayor himself, sitting at his desk, a phone held to his ear.

"Look, I know I told you fifteen girls, but we hit a minor speed bump." There's a pause as he listens to whoever is on the other side of the phone. Probably who he is delivering these girls too. "Yes, yes, a speed bump. My guy was picking up the last girl, but he never showed at the drop point." Another pause. He is either talking about me or Ali. The asshole who attacked me said he told his boss of the change in girls. "No, I don't think he ran off with her, since I've seen her around town." Pause. I really hate not hearing both sides. "Don't worry, I have a plan." Another pause as he chuckles at whatever the person said. "Yes, yes. The cargo is being kept in the fun house until your men set up."

Fun house? The girls are already at the carnival. I need to let the guys know. We can get the girls out and then take out this asshole. I'm about to step away to send a message to the guys when the floor creaks behind me. Large thick arms wrap around my chest in a tight hold, lifting me slightly, so my feet dangle, before shoving me forward and into the mayor's office. The ape of a man behind me releases his hold and I drop to the ground. "Ah, the last of the girls have arrived, just in time. You will like this one, she's...unique and very feisty. You'll have fun breaking her." My eyes snap up to meet a pair of shit brown ones. The mayor gives me a sinister smirk before ogling my body, disgusting lust filling his eyes as he goes. "Ah, indeed." He lets out a deep chuckle, licking his lips as I shudder in repulsiveness as I try to subtly look for my phone that must have dropped when I was grabbed. "See you then." He hangs standing from his desk as he walks towards me.

Sneering up at him. "You're a disgusting pig!" Slap. The bastard's hand lands across my cheek, sending my head flying to the side as I cry out. "You hit like a girl." I spit at his shoes. I'm taken by surprise when I feel a kick to my stomach, leaving me gasping for air. Blood tasting of copper fills in my mouth, so I spit that at him next. "Pussy."

He leans down and pinches my chin, yanking my head up at an awkward angle. "You have a mouth on you, little girl. The man who is buying you is going to have all sorts of fun breaking you. He loves when they fight." I laugh, I let it all out, all my crazy as I grin up at him.

"You fucked up now. They are coming for you. You're going to die tonight." I laugh louder as he slaps me again. He really does hit like a girl.

"No one is coming for me. I'm untouchable." Letting out a nervous chuckle, he stands, straightening his suit as he goes. "Take her and put her with the others."

"The Heathens are coming for you!" I push myself up to stand or maybe fight, but a sudden boot to the head stops me. Pain burst through my skull as I collapsed to the ground, my vision going blurry. I spot my phone that must have slid under the mayor's desk and smile to myself. "My Heathennnnsss." I whisper, knowing they will come for me. I finally allow the darkness to consume me, knowing when I wake, I'll be painting this town red.

Chapter Twenty-Eight

Dante

I hate this, hate not being able to be with her right now. What if something happens? She doesn't have the skills or years of practice to protect herself. The men we are sent after to kill aren't good men and we just allowed her to enter the lion's den without us.

"D, she will be fine. She is going to take a few pictures and maybe look through a few drawers. I told her not to take any unnecessary risks. Kitten can do this. Now finish getting ready so we can do our part. The sooner we get all this done, the sooner we get our woman back in our bed." Chase slaps me on the back before heading out. Probably to go find food. I stare down at the clothes we all picked out. We decided all black was best, so we can blend into the shadows.

I quickly dress, pushing my thoughts and worry aside for now before scooping up my mask to find the others. I find the guys in the kitchen, August playing on his tablet, doing what he does, trying to find any last-minute issues that could arise. Chase, on the other hand, is stuffing his face in a bowl of cereal. The man can eat but not gain a single pound. It could be because he is either eating or working out, so the two activities balance each other out.

"Anything new?" Heading to the fridge to grab a bottle of water.

August is our tech guy, so I know he can probably hack any camera that might be at or around the carnival. "Unfortunately, I don't think the mayor is working with an amateur." He holds up a hand, stopping my response. "Before you ask, let me explain. I checked this feed each day this week. Cameras are spread out around the outside of the carnival, but nothing inside. Everything has seemed normal until today, when all the feeds seem to malfunction."

"So, what you're saying is we don't have eyes on anything?" I finish chugging my water, tossing the empty bottle in the trash.

"Yeah, but they weren't going to help us inside, anyway." He shrugs, saying, what are you gonna do?

"Then let's get down there, get the lay of the land, then see if Trinity found anything useful. If not, we hang tight and keep an eye on the mayor. We know it's happening tonight, so it will only be a matter of time until he leads up to the operation."

Both nod before gathering our things. We packed extra weapons, many already concealed under our clothes. I have several Glocks and a few knives tucked away. I'm sure the guys are packing just as much as me, if not more, since I prefer my fists. You never know when you'll need to fight for your life. Tonight is different, though. I'm fighting for someone else's life as well.

When we get to the Halloween carnival, people are just arriving. Everyone is dressed up in costumes since it was a mandatory suggestion. Families mill about, chasing after kids running booth to booth, playing games, and eating treats. Most families come early to avoid the older crowd that comes later, then leave to party the night away. All oblivious to the fact that their beloved mayor is selling their children to sick and twisted perverts. People only want to see what they want to see and believe what they want to believe.

"Masks on boys. Eyes open. Meet back in front in 30." Sliding our masks over our faces, we start by splitting up, each taking an area of the carnival. I head for the back where the fun house, merry-go-round, and a few other rides sit. As I orbit each ride, the vibrant sounds of music and laughter echo in my ears. I keep a watchful eye on the tree line and surrounding areas for anything suspicious. It's hard to see anything amiss when everyone around is disguised as something else.

I try to watch for figures that could conceal weapons like myself. Surely the mayors' men or the traffickers would be armed for the trade. You can't trust anyone these days, including a business partner.

After a few passes, I head back towards the front to meet the guys. Cupcake should be here any minute. Seeing her will calm this uneasy feeling I've had since getting here. I keep my eyes open and alert, spotting a few shady characters milling about, but nothing screams at me they are a threat. Small towns are full of shady perverts who would get a kick out of watching little kids at a carnival. For all I know, they are here to get their rocks off watching kids. Equally as bad, but I have bigger fish to fry tonight. Maybe I'll plant a seed in Cupcake's mind that she should have a little fun before we leave town. To hone a few skills, I'm sure she knows all the sick pervs around here.

When I reach the entrance, I spot both my brothers, wearing the same mask as me, but each lighting up a different color. I look around them, hoping to spot my Cupcake standing there, but see no one else. I frown before pulling out my phone, checking the time as well as for any miss calls. When I see I received nothing, no SOS or I'm on my way, the uneasy feeling I had earlier intensifies. I waste no time when I finally reach my brothers. "Where is she?" I snarl, like an untamed beast. My grip on my phone tightens, causing it to creak under my hold.

Chase holds up his hands. "D, calm down. She's only a few minutes late. I'm sure she will be walking her sexy ass up to us in no time." He sends me a grin before turning to stare out at the parking lot, but I saw the worry in his eyes he was trying to hide. He looks like a lost puppy waiting for its owner.

"Something's wrong." I say. Searching the parking lot as well, but my gut is telling me she won't be showing up. "I can feel it." And I can. Deep down in my cold, dark heart, Trinity made a place for herself, like she is a part of me now. My gut is telling me to go to her and it has never been wrong before.

"I agree brother." August steps up next to me, pulling out his own phone before frantically typing. His fingers fly over his small screen as he looks for something. "Her phone is pinging at the mayor's office." His face shifts, a hard, determined expression falling in place as he pockets his phone.

I don't bother saying anything as I head for our car, footsteps following like I knew they would. My brothers are just as obsessed with my Cupcake as me. We all pile in before I throw the vehicle into drive. "Let's go find our woman, boys."

259

CHAPTER TWENTY-NINE

TRINITY

"Ughh..." Groaning, I roll to the side, peeking an eyelid open just a sliver. Blinding light temporarily causes me to grimace. My head suddenly feels like a stampede of wild horses running through it. I'm going to kill the bastard that kicked me in the fucking head. I take a few more deep breaths, feeling the tension in my body slowly dissipate, before squinting open my eyes a bit more. Blinking a few times to clear my vision, I focus on my surroundings more.

I realize I'm laid out on my back as my eyes make contact with a metal looking ceiling. Slowly, sounds around me filter in. Soft music and low, deep voices murmuring to my left, while a whimper catches my attention to the right. My body hurts all over, making me think the asshole who knocked me out probably dropped me like a piece of trash, but I manage to roll my head to the right. My eyes widened at seeing a line of girls around my age and younger sitting against a wall. Each looking battered and bruised or possibly drugged but all alive, which is something.

I roll my head to the left next, two guys sit at a small table in the corner, each with a beer in hand. Both men look semi familiar, which means they probably work for the mayor or live in town. I watch them for a minute as they speak back and forth, playing a game of cards, not bothering to look in our direction.

I do a mental full body check, not wanting them to know I'm awake just yet. Flexing my feet, fingers, and everything else I could move discreetly to not to alert the men. Everything feels fine but sore. I take in the rest of the room. The room has four plain metal walls with what looks like a door next to the men, but no handle. Odd. The area where the girls are has a few buckets, ragged blankets, and a couple gallons of water. The bare minimum, since women are simply cattle to these vile men.

Since I see nothing else in the room, I focus back on what I think is the door. The fact that I see no knob, I assume the only way out is if someone from the other side opens it. So much for an easy way out. Knowing that the guys will find me at some point, I need to focus on the here and now. And right now, I really want a nice hot bath. Making a mental note that the guys owe me, I decide to finally get the asshole's attention.

"Ahhh, which one of you assholes threw me in here?" I sit up, placing a hand on my head as it spins for a second, before turning and facing idiot one and idiot two. With their full attention now on me and my new vantage point, I see that the guys each have a gun. So, odds are not in my favor, but never underestimate an underdog.

"Shut up, bitch or I'll make sure you're knocked out longer." Idiot one says. Both guys are wearing dark clothes like my guys tonight. The jerk who spoke looks like he could be in a biker gang. Tattoos, face piercing and a bald head. He sends me a leering look. "You know, the boss said not to touch you but I know of a way to shut you up." Licking his chapped lips, he reaches down, cupping his junk. Gag. "If you know what I mean."

"You must be the dipshit who knocked me out." I stretch out my muscles, knowing I'm about to do something stupid. "And I like real men, not a tiny dick, pea brain idiot who couldn't find a g-spot even if he was given a map." I smirk back, knowing I'm provoking him. A small gasp sounds from behind me, but I refuse to take my eyes off these guys. He reacts just like I thought as he abruptly stands, his chair crashing to the floor, making some girls let out small shrieks.

"You want to talk shit, bitch? I'll show you how a real man fucks." Idiot two stands then, grabbing hold of idiot one's shoulder, holding him back.

"Johnny, calm down. I think you gave her brain damage with that kick to the head. She will get what's coming to her." Johnny glares down at me.

"Yeah, Johnny boy. Sit down like the good dog you are." I let out a crazy laugh as he rips his shoulder away from the second man's grip and charged towards me. This time I'm ready. This time, he isn't coming from behind. When he is within range leaning in to grab for me, I kick up and out. My foot collides with his face, the crunch of his nose breaking is music to my ears as this time he cries out. I don't waste time. Jumping up, I reach for his gun tucked into his waistband. Not having much experience with anything but a knife, my finger hits the trigger as I fumble to get a grip. A shot sounds off, making Johnny grunt as a bullet hits his thigh. Big baby.

Evil man number 2 races forward, swinging his fist towards my head. I step back to avoid the hit, losing grip on the gun as it falls to the floor. A fist slams into my face, causing me to go flying to the floor with my own grunt of pain. My rage and annoyance at being hit multiple times tonight builds, but this time I don't fight it like I have in the past. This time I let it out. Guy 2 must think I'm down for the count, because he turns his back to me as he kneels down to check on his buddy. That's when I see the blade clipped to the back of his pants. Like a gift from above, practically twinkling under the dull fluorescent lights.

I lunge forward, yanking the blade out of its sleeve before slamming it back down into the guy's back. My lips tip up in a grin as I embrace this new side of me. I don't stop as I continue to drag the blade in and out of the man's flesh. Blood splatters my face and body, my arms screaming from the exhaustion. Stab, stab, stab. His thrusting slows to a stop as he slumps forward. Sliding my eyes to the first guy, blood running down his face as he holds his leg, his eyes widen in horror. I must be quite a sight.

"Weren't you going to show me how a real man fucks?" Tilting my head, letting my eyes drift to his crotch, I get an idea. "Pull it out." Somehow, his eyes widened further. "Pull it out and I'll let you live." With shaky hands, he slowly pulls his tiny cock free. I lean forward to inspect it. It sort of reminds me of a baby worm or maggot. *Gross.* Fast as lightning, I snap my hand out, grabbing his dick and swipe the blade down swiftly. A second later, the screaming begins as I hold a bloody, small, wrinkly dick in my hand. "Oops." I toss the shriveled dick aside. "My hand slipped." Shrugging, I turn to check on the girls. They all stare at me in fear and maybe awe. I'm sure these assholes fucked with them at some point.

The screaming continues mixed with snot filled tears as the man now holds his dickless crotch. "Oh, shut up, bitch." My knife slips again as I embed it into Johnny boy's chest. The screams and sobs finally end as I turn back to the terrified women. "Well, looks like now we wait."

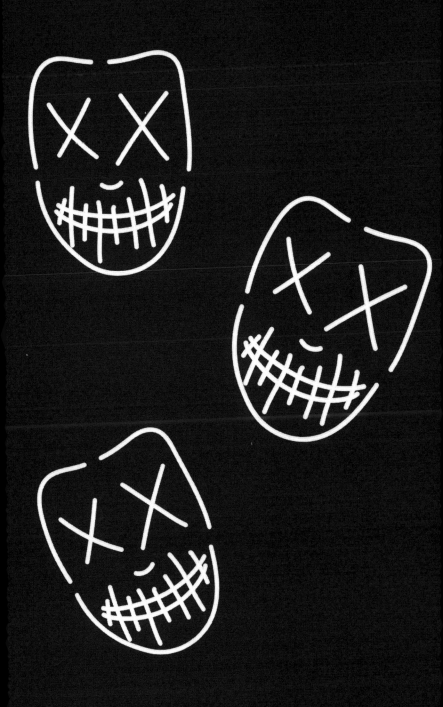

Chapter Thirty

Chase

I have always trusted Dante's gut. It's saved us a time or two, but a part of me is really hoping he is wrong this time. I went over everything I could think of that would be helpful for Kitten to sneak around. We even watched spy movies to set the mood. Though a few of those times we didn't get very far into the movie to learn anything useful. I learned a lot during those times, like how Kitten Screams out in pleasure when you fuck her from behind and hit that certain spot or how the woman is basically a hoover vacuum cleaner when sucking cock. I try to stay positive. Maybe she is purposefully taking her time to fuck with us. The moment the thought comes to mind, I dismiss it. She wants to take down these assholes just as much as we do. She's been prepped, primed and ready for days.

I got a glance at her when she left her house. It wasn't enough, but I saw she had a painted face and splashes of color everywhere. I noticed she stayed true to herself with a pair of black Converses to go with her outfit. My Kitten is a dime a dozen because while most girls her age are dressed half naked, she is dressed ready for battle. I would be lying if I said I didn't want to peel that outfit off her, lay her across my bed, and have my wicked way with her.

My dirty thoughts are interrupted as Dante pulls up to the town hall, throwing the car into park, then jumping out without warning. He doesn't wait for either me or August as he beelines it to the front doors. No one should be here since the sun has set and the Halloween carnival was in full swing when we were pulling out. D makes quick work of picking the lock and within minutes, we are in and heading straight for the mayor's office. When we get to the end of the hall, D pauses, putting his ear to the door to listen. He must not hear anything as he pulls out his lock picking set again and gets to work.

Once in, we don't speak as we look through drawers, filing cabinets and anywhere else someone could hide secrets. The room is a decent size for a small-town mayor's office. A large oak desk sits on one side of the room, with a huge wingback chair you might see in an evil villain's lair sitting just behind it. An additional two leather chairs sit across from the front. The desk itself holds a computer, name plate and stacks of random papers. The walls are a pale beige color, a large window looking out toward the woods giving an amazing view. Against the far wall holds a huge self portrait of the fat bastard attempting to look regal or more well off than people would think. Really, the entire room says, *Hi, I'm a douche. Nice to meet you.*

"He has her, I know it. Find anything that might point to where he holds the girls. He wanted her last week, so I'm guessing he still wants her now." D says, as he flings open drawers, emptying the contents, losing all pretense of being sneaky. I head straight for the wall, looking for any seams in the walls or picture frames with hinges. A man like this must have a small safe, hidden shelf or a false wall. Dragging my hands along the wooden walls, my eyes drift around the room until I spot a small dark spot on the rug. Kneeling down, I swipe my finger through the stain, grimacing a bit when my finger touches something wet. Pulling bac,k I see red, quickly rubbing my fingers together and determining that it's… "Blood."

"What?" August kneels next to me, repeating what I had done, nodding up at Dante, who is now clenching his fist and grinding his teeth. He turns, punching the wall nearest him.

"I knew this was a stupid fucking idea. Why the fuck did we let her do this?! Now that sick fuck has her and we still don't have the information we need." D has turned into a snarling beast as he more forcefully rips out drawers and searches through papers.

"We could just find him and kill him." I call out, looking around again, feeling like I'm missing something important. My eyes catch on a lump just under the large desk. I crawl towards it, my hands wrapping around a small black device. Turning it on, I see the smiling face of my Kitten. "Kitten!" Jumping to my feet, I turn to August, our tech guy, thrusting the small phone into his chest.

"Wh-" His words cut off as he realized what I meant. Quickly getting to work, as he opens apps. Dante joins me as we wait impatiently for Aug to find something useful. "You smart girl." His eyes snap up to us. "She recorded something a little while ago." We listen intently as August plays back what he found.

"Don't worry, I have a plan."

"Yes, yes. The cargo is being kept in the fun house until your men show up."

"Ah, the last of the girls have arrived, just in time. You will like this one, she's…unique and very feisty. You'll have fun breaking her." I'm going to kill him. Maybe get medieval on his ass and gut him before hanging him off a bridge.

"He probably took her to the funhouse. Let's go!" D turns to leave and I go to follow when August stops us.

"Wait, there is more." He holds the phone up and frowns.

"You're a disgusting pig!" The sound of a slap rings loud before Kitten cries out. I clench my fist, thoughts of ways to make this asshole suffer filling my mind.

"You hit like a girl." Another slap. "Pussy." That's my girl. Sassy until the end.

"You have a mouth on you, little girl. The man who is buying you is going to have all sorts of fun breaking you. He loves when they fight."

"I'm going to kill him nice and slow." D growls, his features turn to hard stone.

Laughter fills the air, making me grin. "You fucked up now. They are coming for you. You're going to die tonight." Kitten laughs harder, making my chest fill with pride.

"No one is coming for me. I'm untouchable. Take her and put her with the others." I can hear light footsteps walking around before we can hear again Trinity.

"The Heathens are coming for you!" A loud thump followed by a louder thump, like a body hitting the ground, has my heart dropping out of my chest. Panic increases my heart rate as I look up at the guys. Similar looks stare back at me before a soft, weak whisper fills the silence. "My Heathennnnsss." That simple plea breaks me. No one says a thing as we turn and rush from the room.

Hang on Kitten, we're coming for you!

We make it back to the carnival in record time. A single destination in mind, the funhouse. Entering the carnival this time feels different as we each slide our masks into place. "Welcome to the carnival. We're closing in about 30 minutes, but a few rides and stands are still open." A woman dressed as a slutty witch calls out. I hadn't even realized the sun went down or how late it had gotten.

"Keep your eyes open. With this place closing soon, I'm sure the mayor's guys will start putting the trade in place." D, at the front, calls out as we make a straight shot to the back of the carnival grounds.

"How are we playing this? Shoot first, ask questions later? Or quiet and sneaky?" Rubbing my hands together in anticipation, I dart my gaze around. The witch was right, as I watch vendors close up shops. It's odd because you would think with it being a holiday, they would keep this place open late. I guess selling bodies makes more money than selling cotton candy. It's not long until we reach our destination, heading right for the entrance. We bypass a sign saying 'closed for repairs' and find ourselves in a room with flashing lights. It's almost like a disco with an actual disco ball on the ceiling, causing the lights to seem blinding.

"Weapons out. It's no coincidence there was a closed sign. This is a funhouse, so I'm guessing we are going to run into weird shit. Keep an eye out for any hidden doors or rooms." D pulls his Glock out before loading one into the chamber. "If we run into anyone, shoot first." He turns back towards the next hall, and I crack my neck, hyping myself up. I love a good shoot first game. "Let's go find our woman."

It feels like forever and like we've gone in twenty circles. Each room is unique with bright colors, moving parts, blinding lights. It's all disorienting and hard to focus. We move into another moving room; this one is all optical illusions with a shifting floor. For a place that is supposed to be closed for repairs, it sure is working just fine. I'm starting to get a headache with all the twists and turns the room is making. "I think I'm going to be sick. There has to be an easier way to find her than wandering through this madhouse." I lean against a wall, closing my eyes to calm my brain.

"We have to keep going. We just need to find some sort of door." I mentally roll my eyes because it's like finding a needle in a haystack right now. Taking a deep breath, I turn my head to tell August just that when I spot a raised bump on the wall. Stepping towards it, I run my hand along until I feel what we were looking for. I skim my fingers up and around the small, barely noticeable seam before pressing into the center. A push release door clicks open, revealing a second hidden door.

"Bingo." This door has a padlock on it, and before I can mention it, Dante is shoving me out of the way with his picking tools already in hand. Making quick work again, the lock pops open, and D is swinging the door wide, gun at the ready. August and I rush in behind him, prepared for a shootout but find a small metal room covered in red. My eyes shift all around, trying to spot my blond hair feisty kitten. Across the way, a group of girls huddled together, all half naked, filthy with grime and dirt. In the center of the room, two men lay on the ground, blood pooling around them. They look like a rabid beast tore through them. One guy lies on his back, pants pulled slightly down, crotch soaked in blood; next to him, a flaccid cock.

"What the-"

"Took you guys long enough! I thought I was actually going to have to use that nasty bucket." A feminine, sultry voice calls out. Movement from the darkened corner to my left causes me to turn. Gun raised at the ready before a goddess of death splattered in blood steps into the dull light, smirking. I damn near fall to my knees to worship this woman as her eyes light with relief and satisfaction.

"Kitten!"

CHAPTER THIRTY-ONE

AUGUST

When we entered the small room, guns were ready. This completely caught me off guard. I figured the girls would be surrounded by poor conditions, cowering in a corner, sobbing messes but the bloody massacre in the middle of the room never crossed my mind. I watch as Chase rushes forward, scooping Trinity up in a tight hold before slamming his lips down on hers. Taking this second to take in her appearance, I spot blood splatter all over her face. If you didn't know better, you might think it was a part of her costume. For the most part, she looks okay, but the sound we heard over the phone still plays in my head. The slapping of skin, pained grunts and then a final thump before it went quiet. Hearing that made my heart race, fear that we might not get her back.

"Cupcake, what happened?" Dante's worried demeanor washes away the moment he sees her safe. The stoney bastard pretending like he wasn't the most panicked when we find her missing. He's not fooling me as he kneels down to inspect our girl's handy work, never really looking away from her.

"Apparently, they never forgot about me. I was still a target, so when I showed up, I overheard the mayor talking on the phone about a shipment." Darting her eyes towards the wide-eyed girls, trying to blend into the back wall. "I got closer to record everything when he mentioned the funhouse. I was moving away, about to call you and get out of there, when that asshole grabbed me." She nods down to the dickless man, making me grimace.

"Remind me never to piss you off, Kitten." Chase covers his junk in fear like any man would.

"I would never. I enjoy the sex too much." She gives him a wink. "Unless you try to stick your dick somewhere else, then I might." He shakes his head, eyes going wide at the glee he sees in hers. "Anyway, the mayor slapped me around a few times." Lowering her voice, she whisper shouts. "He didn't like me calling him a pussy." She shrugs like it was nothing. "His henchmen gave me a boot to the face, knocking me out. I woke up here, then I got bored with waiting for you guys and decided to get rid of these two."

Crossing his arms and stomping his foot like a child, Chase pouts. "Bad Kitten! You started playing without me?!" She just rolls her eyes at his theatrics.

"So, what now?" She frowns, taking in the girls again. "We can't let them be taken." She turns pleading eyes to us.

"We need to deal with the mayor and his guys first. We shouldn't move them without knowing what is going on outside. I can-" As if the universe is speaking to us, the fun house lights go out. The girls against the wall let out high-pitched screams as emergency backup lights flash on. Dante is now next to Trinity, standing over her like a protective pit bull.

"Let's get moving. I bet that's a sign someone is getting ready to pick up their cargo." D calls out as he heads to the door. Trinity approaches the girls, hands raised in a non-threatening manner. It's like she is attempting to approach a wild animal as she slowly squats to be more on their level.

"Hey. I know you're all scared, but I need you to stay as quiet as you can. Whatever you hear, ignore it. Stay here until I come and get you. Do you understand?" Her voice is low, calm as she speaks. Most of the girls won't even lift their eyes, but the few that do nod in understanding. "Good. August, grab me one of the dead guy's guns." I do as she says, check the mags and put one in the chamber before handing it over to her. "Do any of you know how to use a gun?" One girl gives a small, barely noticeable nod. "Good. Point and shoot anyone that comes through that door. Except me, don't shoot me. I'll call out when it's safe. Okay?" The girl still says nothing as she scoots forward to the front, grabbing the gun with shaky hands. "Good. Remember to stay quiet." With nothing else left to say, we head to where D and Chase wait by the door.

Before we reach them, she bumps my arm, gaining my attention. "I knew you would come for me."

"Always Little Muse, always."

"Let's split into two teams. The carnival is probably closed by now, so if anyone is around, they aren't the good guys. Try to keep it to quiet kills. Our job's not done and we don't get paid unless the target is confirmed dead." Dante is now in full mission mode. He looks at me before nodding to Trinity, letting me know I'm with her. We waste no more time as we make our way back into the funhouse, shutting and securing the door as we leave. This time, the fun house maze is easier to maneuver as we head for the exit.

We all make quick work getting outside since this place has only one way in and out. Before we turn the corner to fresh air, we all pause. Silence builds with tension as no one says a thing, but so many things should be said right now. I can hear indistinct murmurs heading in our direction so Chase being who he is, cutting the tension like a knife to butter. "Whoever has the most kills gets Kitten all to themselves tonight. Extra points if you kill the mayor. Ready, set, go!"

Chase takes off like a horse out the gate, ducking low to peek around the corner before jetting forward.

Dante and I let out deep sighs while Trinity lets out a giggle. "I still don't know how the guy is still alive today." Dante reaches out, hands tangling in her hair, as he leans in. "You best believe you'll be in my bed tonight, Cupcake." Then he's fucking her mouth with his tongue. It's a short, quick kiss, filled with passion before he is turning away, storming after our crazy brother.

"Well, we can't let these guys win." She sends me a wink, heading for the exit, and I follow like the smitten puppy in love that I am. When we reach the entrance, it's quiet, with no sign of the guys or anyone else, for that matter. I nod for her to follow me to the side. I figured we could make our way around and towards the front to make our way back. We're quiet as we skim the edge of booths and vendors when, out of nowhere, the sound of a gunshot can be heard. Forgetting about our own safety, we rush towards the deafening sound, rounding a corner to find a guy wearing a clown costume has been shot. A gun in his hand shows he wasn't a nice clown, so good riddance.

"There's four of them. Find them now, but keep the bitch alive." I yank Trinity down behind a booth by her arm with one hand while using the other to cover her mouth. Her chest is rising and falling rapidly as I shift us further back. Bringing my finger to my lips, I make a hush motion before removing my hand over her mouth and grabbing my gun.

Footsteps stop not too far away from our position. "Boss, they killed Don." In a flash, my Little Muse is moving. Leaping forward, knife in hand, she grips the new man's hair in a fist, then slices her blade across his throat. Gurgling noises sound out, the man reaching up to stop the bleeding but she didn't hesitate with the cut, making it deep. The sounds die out after a second and he falls to the ground next to his dead friends as she grins down at me.

"I have three kills already, counting the two in the holding room." She tosses her thumb behind her, indicating the fun house. "Those totally count, by the way." Trinity wipes the blood covered knife on the dead guy's clothes, turning towards me with a wicked grin. "Let's make our own bet." Cocking a brow in question, I take a second to survey the area. We are sitting ducks here, but I can't deny this woman her fun.

"What kind of bet?" I keep my gun in hand. We agreed on quiet but the fact both these guys have guns, I don't want to take any chances.

"Whoever has the lower body count has to sit as the others nude model for a painting session." The sneaky minx. She knew I wouldn't be able to resist something like this.

"Deal, Little Muse. Let's play."
And then she's off.

CHAPTER THIRTY-TWO

TRINITY

I bob and weave my way through the empty carnival, trying to find targets to sink my blade into. I know the last few weeks should have freaked me out or even sent me to some type of psych ward, but I can't deny it all feels right. The guys, the sex, the blood, the way my knife finds home inside someone's body. I hear August trailing behind attempting to keep up, but I'm small and can move faster. I finally come across two men shining flashlights toward the trees, back to me. Taking a deep breath, my steps become light as I head for the guy closest to me. This guy unfortunately isn't kneeling so, doing a little running jump, I cling to the man's back like a koala as I stab, stab, stab at his chest. He attempts to swing me off, but I hold tight. The grunts he makes attracts his partner's attention next. This guy raises his gun, but my man is faster. A shot rings out as guy number two drops to the ground, a new hole in his head.

"That was one hell of a shot." The man I'm clinging to finally drops to his knees, allowing my feet to finally touch the ground as I shove him forward. The handsome bastard just winks before moving on, a clear sign he is now playing to win.

We continue on making a sweep of the grounds. We both killed a few more along the way, but there was no telling how many guys there were in total. "Let's regroup with the guys. There can't be that many left." Knowing I'll follow, we make our way back through the booths and vendors towards the house of horrors. I mean fun house. We were just passing a cotton candy vendor stand when I saw a shadow shift to my right, making me pause as I focused in on the darkness. I know I shouldn't and that the guys are going to be pissed, but this is a game and I want to win. I do the stupid thing and follow the man shaped shadow away from my guys. A part of me knows this is the mayor, from the shadow's shape and the fact he was hiding in the dark while his men got slaughtered. Plus, this coward is heading away from the carnival and towards the beach. I monitor my surroundings as I keep a suitable distance, not wanting this asshole to know about me, so I'm ready.

The figure stops next to the pier before frantically pulling out his phone. "You need to help me. Someone is going around killing my guys."

"What do you mean, you won't help?" The man is still cloaked in semi darkness, making it hard to confirm, but his voice says it all. The mayor. Chase said he was worth a bonus point. "Yes, she called them Heathens, but I thought they were a joke."

"We had a deal. You can't back out of it now. You're already in the area. I just need some of your men. It can't be that hard to kill these guys." The man begins to pace, from nerves or maybe because he knows he's being hunted. That for once he's not the predator but the prey. "Wait, please. I can double the number of girls for half the price. Wait. Hear me ou-" His words cut off as he suddenly threw his phone in anger, cursing up a storm.

"Tsk tsk tsk." I mock, stepping out of my own shadows. "Hello Mr. Mayor." I give him a small wave, knife still in hand.

"You." He turns towards me, fury written all over his face. "You did all this." He opens his arms wide to encase everything I've ruined today. With each step closer, my pleased smile grows wider, expressing my genuine delight. I'm basically the cat that got the cream right now. I've almost reached stabbing distance, the red haze urging me to feed it. To give in to my rage, to everything I've ever been through, the rage I felt when seeing those girls who could have been me or my best friend, my anger at all the girls who have already been lost. I let it all consume me, fueling the fire burning in my chest.

"Well, someone had to, but this was a long time coming. Men like you, who think they can use and abuse women any way they see fit, make me sick. We women should be cherished, worshiped. Only women can give life, but we can also take it away." Like letting a wild creature free for the first time in years, I move, racing forward those last few feet. This time the red haze consumes me fully, like I'm a whole different person, or watching it from the outside. With each passing moment, I feel myself becoming more untamed, unleashing a newfound sense of freedom.

"I won fair and square. It's not my fault you three are sore losers. Plus, Chase is the one who claimed the prime target was worth double points." Sticking my tongue out at the three grown men pouting on the couch.

I'm still covered in blood, but so glad for this night to be over. Luckily, the guys set up an aftermath plan that included bringing in the FBI to clean up our mess. They said they knew someone who they could trust and gave him all the information to pursue further. After I made the mayor unrecognizable, I stopped at the fun house and explained what was going on. Most of the girls are probably traumatized but hopefully not so much they can't be saved. We informed them outside law enforcement were coming in and to not trust their towns. Many of the girls come from the surrounding towns and states, but we still have no idea how deep this could have gone. We told them to stay put until the FBI showed up giving them a codeword. I also asked them to leave me out of it, but the guys assured me they took care of everything.

Now we're here. Sitting in their living room arguing over who technically won. Me, of course, but men are big babies, refusing to admit defeat.

"Alright Kitten. Even though you cheated, we will let you think you won, but now you have to pick who you want for the night."

Tapping my finger to my chin, I consider my answer, taking in each guy. "Why can't I have all of you again?" Blinking up at them with big, innocent eyes. I slowly peel off my now sticky with dried blood costume. Sinfully sexy smirks appear on their faces as they side-eye each other. "I have one request. Keep the masks on."

"You naughty little devil. I like the way you think." Chase licks his lips before letting out a low, deep groan.

Dante, on the other hand, readjusted himself before pulling me onto his lap, forcing my thighs wide to straddle his hips. "You were a queen of the night, the goddess of death and absolutely glorious tonight, Cupcake." Another set of hands cup my cheeks, turning my face as Dante lowers his head to my neck. Apparently, none of us really care that we are all still covered in blood. My eyes meet the soulful pair of August, his eyes shifting all over my body.

"I have to say Little Muse, red looks damn good on you."

Epilogue- Trinity

The following weeks, the Heathens completed their jobs were a whirlwind. The first few days are fuzzy because of the endless sex haze I was in after we got home. If we weren't one big orgy, I would be riding one or another, would be having his dessert before fucking me to sleep. It was an endless cycle that I wasn't mad about. I was sore for a week, having to put a week ban on any funny business until I could walk straight again.

Once I wasn't high of lust, the guys bought the topic of me leaving town with them. I was against it at first, not wanting to leave Gran all alone, but when she found out my reasoning, the woman taped an eviction notice to my bedroom door; stating I had 2 weeks to vacate the property or she would turn me into the police. I knew it was an empty threat, but coming home the next day to the front door locks being changed. Made me realize she really wanted me gone. We both knew I wanted to leave this town eventually, but I was stalling for her. She let me, knowing I struggled to hide my darker side, but somehow, she knew I would find someone to help balance me; or someone's. The guys assured me she would be well taken care of and that I could come to visit whenever I wanted.

"Are you almost ready, Cupcake? We need to head out soon. Boss, wanting to meet you in person means you can't be late."

"Yeah, I just need to get dressed." I call out as I knot the towel across my chest before heading back to the room. The moment my foot hits the carpet, I freeze. My three Heathens are standing at the end of the bed all in different stages of undress. "I thought we needed to leave soon. Why are you all in here?" Each one of their eyes traces the lingering drops of water as they race down my body. "Eyes up here, boys."

"No, I think I prefer this look on you. Naked, wet, and oh so ready." Chase reaches down, readjusting his thick cock as it outlines his dark jeans. He doesn't have a shirt on, so his array of ink is on display, drawing my eyes to his chest.

"I have to agree, brother. Just a small tug could see it all." Dante reaches forward, causing me to step back. "Wouldn't you like that Cupcake?" I tighten my hand over the knot as my core cries out in need. My body wants them, but my brain knows we have things that we have to do.

"Little Muse, D asked you a question. Wouldn't you like to bear for us?" I glare at my usually well-mannered boyfriend. He simply cocks a brow, knowing I'm going to give in any way.

"Maybe, but we need to get ready to leave. I prefer to not piss off my new boss." The men all share a glance before moving to circle me. Fingers float across my skin, causing me to shiver in anticipation.

"I think we have time for a quicky." Chase darts in, running his nose up my neck, taking in a deep inhale. "You smell so sweet, Kitten. I need a taste." As I'm focusing on Chase and his movements, one of the others yanks my towel away, leaving me open for the guys to appraise.

"Relax Cupcake. This is more important than the boss, now on the bed. Spread them." Dante steps to the side allowing me access to our California King sized bed, as he rips his shirt up and over his head. Deciding to be a good girl for once, I lay myself out, legs spread wide as my men approach undressing as they go.

"Now, your Lover Boy is going to taste that sweet pink pussy while prepping that juicy ass for August here. While he's doing that, you're going to open that pretty mouth and let me fuck it nice and hard." My chest rises and falls rapidly as my heart rate picks up. Dante knows how wet I get when he talks like this. This is how he got his nickname, Lucifer, after all. Chase wasted no time diving in, his tongue giving me long firm licks as he gathered my juices for lube, sliding his finger lower to prep my ass for August.

The bed dips next to my head as Dante leans forward, his face becoming my entire view. "Be a good girl and scream our names loud enough our neighbors will hear." He descends, his lips colliding with mine as Chase devours my core. Hands glide across my skin, making intricate designs as they climb to my breast, giving them a squeeze before a hot mouth finds my nipple.

Dante breaks the kiss, shifting into position as I turn my head, opening my mouth wide in his direction. A moan slips free as Chase sucks my clit, slowly inserting a finger into my ass. A second later, a cock is cutting off any sounds as it slides to the back of my throat. I swallow, tightening my throat muscles around his cock, his own groan echoing off the walls.

My body is buzzing, a live wire ready to electrocute me into climax as my men suck, lick, grip, pinch, and pound into me. The way these men use me is higher than any kind of drug could give me. Like a tidal wave, a climax so strong my back arches off the bed, my scream soundless around Dante's thick cock hit me. I see stars, super nova's, blinding me before my body comes back to earth.

"She's ready." Like a limp rag doll, I'm lifted as the guys reposition themselves. Chase climbs onto the bed, laying on his back, as I'm placed straddling him. He lines his shaft up, allowing me to slide down at my own smooth, steady pace. Once I'm fully sheathed, a hand to my back presses me down, hands gripping my hips as August lines himself up next. He enters me at a snail's pace, every inch stretching me to the max. "Good little Kitten. Look at you. Taking us so well. You were made for this." Lips walk up my neck with little nibbles and nips as August gets fully settled. I'm so full my body is vibrating with excitement. This is my favorite part, when they all take a hole and fuck me senseless, till my body is sore and my throat is harsh from screaming.

A second before August and Chase start to move, Dante is back, filling my mouth and muting my screams of pleasure. As one they move, fucking me like a needy cat in heat. In and out. In and out. They are relentless, as my core tightens. "Fuck, fuck, fuck. That's its Kitten. She's going to come." Hands tangle through my hair, yanking my head up as my eyes snap open, steel-gray eyes blazing with lust stare back.

"Now." Like the bastards rehearsed it, they all slammed into me at once. Grunts, groans, moans filling my ears as intense pain flares followed by the most incredible pleasure I've ever felt consumes me. I swallow Dante down as hot sprays of cum paint my insides. I'm pretty sure I black out at some point because one by one, each man removes himself as I'm gently laid out on the soft satin sheets.

A warm, wet washcloth cleans up the aftermath of our activities as I keep my eyes closed, officially ready for bed. "I think we are going to be late now." I murmur as I cuddle into the warm body against my back.

"You did good, Cupcake." A hand splays across my stomach. "We can't wait to see you nice and plump with one of our kids. Until then, we plan to worship you every damn day like the queen of heathens you are." I smile at Dante's whispered words as my body relaxes, my mind shutting down as I fade into a sweet and blissful- well fucked- slumber. My last thought is a fitting one.

I think I'll get myself a crown to fit my new title.

ACKNOWLEDGEMENTS

HEY GUYS, I JUST WANT TO TAKE A
SECOND AND SAY THANK YOU TO A FEW
AMAZING LADIES THAT HELPED MAKE
THIS BOOK POSSIBLE!
MELANY A., MELISSA N., AND ASHLEY M.,
THIS BOOK JUST WOULDN'T HAVE BEEN
DONE IN TIME WITHOUT YOU. SO, THANK
YOU! YOU GUYS WERE AWESOME AND
MADE MY LIFE JUST A TAD BIT LESS
STRESSFUL!

ALSO BY N.OWENS

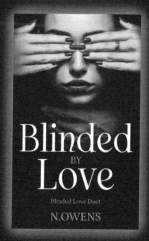

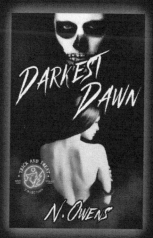

STALK ME
I LIKE IT.

Made in the USA
Middletown, DE
05 November 2023

41864232R00175